THE SAINT

DE WOLFE PACK
THE SERIES

CATHY MACRAE

www.cathymacraeauthor.com

DE WOLFE PACK: THE SERIES

By Alexa Aston
Rise of de Wolfe

By Amanda Mariel
Love's Legacy

By Anna Markland
Hungry Like de Wolfe

By Autumn Sands
Reflection of Love

By Barbara Devlin
Lone Wolfe: Heirs of Titus De Wolfe Book 1
The Big Bad De Wolfe: Heirs of Titus De Wolfe Book 2
Tall, Dark & De Wolfe: Heirs of Titus De Wolfe Book 3

By Cathy MacRae
The Saint

By Christy English
Dragon Fire

By Hildie McQueen
The Duke's Fiery Bride

By Kathryn Le Veque
River's End

By Lana Williams
Trusting the Wolfe

By Laura Landon
A Voice on the Wind

DEDICATION

For my mother,
One of the strongest women I know.

TABLE OF CONTENTS

The Saint

Following in the footsteps of his uncle, the famous Lord William de Wolfe, Geoffrey de Wylde was counted among the greatest knights England had ever known. Revered for his justness and strict adherence to the chivalric code, he was known as *The Saint*.

Fleeing the unwanted attentions of her late husband's brother, Marsaili de Ville runs headlong into the path of The Saint. She wants nothing more than to reach the safety of her family's home in Scotland before Edmund de Ville's henchmen capture her, but Geoffrey de Wylde insists on becoming her protector, slowing her flight and putting her unknowingly at risk.

As her past catches up with her, Marsaili will find more than a safe haven in The Saint's arms. And Geoffrey de Wylde will discover his code does not tell him what to do with a woman who has been accused of murder, yet has captured his heart.

MEDIEVAL GLOSSARY

(A few words I found particularly interesting ~ Cathy)

Bluttering – blurting out (words)

Butter-teeth – top front incisors

Fadoodle – something foolish; nonsense

Fairhead – beauty

Spit-frog – a short sword (perhaps less impressive in size than a battle sword? Of a size to 'spit'—or spear—a frog?)

Wallydraigle – a slovenly, worthless woman

Wench – a woman (this was not viewed as a derogatory term in this era)

CHAPTER ONE

Northern England, 1235 AD

THE SHRILL SOUND of a woman's voice intruded on his thoughts. The woman did not seem to be weeping—and for that he was eternally grateful—but she obviously was not getting her way. And it appeared until she was appeased, he, Lord Geoffrey de Wylde, newly made baron of Galewood, was not going to get *his* way.

He sincerely hoped his knights could settle the issue. The winter wind's cold bite did not encourage him to step from the questionable comfort of his conveyance, but time was slipping past. He should have been away from the inn at least an hour ago.

He drummed his fingertips impatiently on his thigh.

Moments passed. His back had scarcely rested against the thickly padded seat of his covered conveyance when a firm tap registered on the painted doors.

"Yes." He sighed heavily, stifling the bitter word he wouldn't have dreamed of uttering during the past year.

The door cracked open and a wizened face appeared. Sparse gray hair danced in the wind about the weathered head, and worry rounded pale blue eyes.

"M'lord," the man began with a nervous glance over his shoulder.

"Put your cap back on, Wythevede," Geoffrey murmured. "I will not have you catching your death over a caterwauling woman."

Wythevede quickly jammed his thick, knitted cap over his thinning pate and cleared his throat. "M'lord, the female is blocking the way out of the yard." He drew himself up. "De Bretteby and de Ellerton weren't no help."

Geoffrey raised an eyebrow, partly at his driver's familiar use of his knights' names, partly at the thought the two battle-hardened men found themselves unable to manage a single woman long enough for his cart to make its less-than-timely departure. Reaching for the silver-handled cane resting against the corner between the seat and the wall, he rose to his feet, hiding a grimace as his right leg took its share of his weight.

Wythevede wrung his hands. "M'lord, perhaps I could try again . . . ."

Anger darted through Geoffrey at the implication he was less than capable of attending matters, though to be certain, he did not wish to confront a woman who was currently defying his two guards. He let the irritation pass, saving it for the moments ahead.

Bracing against the cane, he lowered himself from the conveyance, taking care not to jar his leg as he reached the ground. He took in the scene before him, ignoring the complaining stab of pain in his thigh as it reminded him his old injury did not care for cold weather.

Voices fell to a low murmur then died away as stable boys caught sight of him. Geoffrey let them look their fill, squaring his shoulders beneath the flap of his heavy black wool cape. He drew his lips into their habitual scowl and settled his gaze on the mud-bespattered young woman causing the ruckus.

Copper-red hair jutted from what may have once been a tight braid, though it must have been combed and plaited hours if not days earlier. She spun toward him, following the others' sudden stare in his direction, and her cheeks pinked slightly under his intense scrutiny. Clear blue eyes widened and she teetered slightly before bracing herself against the shoulder of the horse beside her. The animal shifted his feet and tossed his head, neighing in distress.

Geoffrey glanced at the injured beast, noting the trembling foreleg and the hoof the horse was reluctant to let touch the ground. Then snapped his gaze back to the young woman as she snatched up her skirts and hurried in his direction.

"I need another horse," she stated, her voice taut and matter-of-fact. She waved a hand at the heavily-muscled man standing in the doorway of the stable. "He says he has none. I marked at least three inside this disreputable pile of rubble, and whilst the beasts may not carry me far, they certainly will make it to the next village."

Geoffrey surveyed the woman, his first inclination to dismiss her out of hand as a troublesome chit warring with his innate desire to right the wrong being done.

He shifted his gaze to the stable master who'd provided such good care to his own team of horses the night before. The man crossed his arms over his chest and frowned.

"They aren't mine to offer," he declared, casting a withering look at the woman pleading her case. "Leastwise, not to the likes of her," he muttered.

The woman rounded on him. "Because I dinnae arrive here in a gilded box, dangling from the arm of a wealthy lord?" Her words dripped scorn. "Because ye believe a woman doesnae deserve the same courtesies as a man?" She raised a slender arm, flicking fingers at him in dismissal.

"What say you, milord?" she queried Geoffrey. "Am I of less importance because my legs hide beneath a skirt?"

He disregarded the soft cadence of her speech as memories of the life he'd recently left jumped to the forefront of his mind. "Nay," he said. "'Tis not right to deny a person something that is within your power to give, simply because she is female." He hid a twitch of his lips at the woman's startled look and fought the urge to smile. This a simple case of right and wrong.

"If she has coin to pay for the rental, give her the horse of her choice." He checked the stable master's protest with a glare, the scowl more familiar to the muscles of his face than the smile had been.

"Move milady's horse and clear the path. I am already late." Dismissing the tableau in the yard, he turned and mounted the steps into the cart as large, wet snowflakes swirled through the air and matted against the fabric of his cloak. Giving his two soldiers-at-arms a disgruntled look that promised a reckoning from them later, he slipped into the conveyance.

He sank into the cushioned seat and thumped his cane on the floor. Wythevede scurried up the steps with a freshly heated stone wrapped in a flannel cloth and placed it beneath the fur draped over Geoffrey's lap. Twice the old man caught his breath as though to speak, but Geoffrey warned him off with a look. Taking the hint, the wizened man departed, closing the door behind him.

Gritting his teeth against the throbbing pain in his leg, Geoffrey shifted the stone a bit closer. After a moment, he relaxed, settling deeper into the padded comfort.

He fought the urge to open the panel at the window as he waited for his driver to move the horses forward. Each stamp of a hoof and shake of their shaggy bodies jarred the cart, adding to his growing discomfort. Looking forward to hours cooped up in his 'gilded box' was no more pleasurable than hours astride a saddle, which was where he longed to be. He pushed aside his frustration with the wound in his leg that still had not healed after a year of treatment by eminent physicians, and stared despondently at the empty seat before him.

With a mighty jerk, indicative of the length of time they'd remained stationery as the wooden wheels broke free of the accumulated snow and ice, the conveyance lurched forward. Geoffrey snared the edge of the panel with the tip of his cane and lowered it a few inches, disappointed to see nothing more than an empty yard, the mud and muck rapidly disappearing beneath a growing mantle of white.

LADY MARSAILI DE Ville wiped her trembling hands on her grimy skirts, hating the feel of days-old mud and grit ground into the fabric. She also hated feeling cold, hunted and exhausted, though she'd endure the cold and exhaustion over the sure knowledge of what would happen to her if her late husband's conniving brother caught up with her.

"I'll take the bay," she stated, lifting a haughty brow at the stable master.

The man swore aloud, apparently sufficiently cowed by the nobleman who'd come to her assistance to give her the horse, but not liking the situation one damn bit. With a jerk of his head, he sent a stable boy scurrying into the stable, returning moments later with the animal in question.

"You'll have to use yer own saddle," the stable master informed her bluntly. "I'll not put my good tack on the beast knowing how you'll abuse it." He nodded pointedly to the mud-caked saddle on Marsaili's horse.

"Fair enough," she replied, striding forward to remove the saddle herself. It was the cursed weather, not ill-use that covered the horse and tack, but she wasn't about to argue the point.

An elderly man hobbled to her side and patted the edge of her cloak. "M'lady, could we not give yer beast a chance to heal?" He glanced at the sky now billowing with snowflakes, stark white against the grey clouds.

Marsaili jerked the strap securing the saddle, battling tears of frustration as her fingers slipped on the damp leather. She clawed angrily at the stubborn knot, refusing to give in to the horror her life had become.

"We have no time, Hew. Ye know what will happen if Edmund finds us." She snatched her hand back, biting down on a finger. Pulling the digit from her mouth, she eyed the nail critically.

"Damn! Stubborn thing! I broke a nail." Giving her hand a shake, she attacked the saddle girth with renewed vigor, ignoring the frigid air that crept into every seam of her clothing, deadening skin and enthusiasm alike.

With heady triumph, she at last pulled the girth free. Hew sidled closer and helped her pull the weighty saddle from her tired mount's back and set it atop the bay.

"'Tis not fit weather for man nor beast, if'n ye dinnae mind my saying so." Hew gave a long-suffering sniff. Straightening the stirrup leather, he eyed his mistress.

Marsaili laid a palm on his sleeve. "Ye dinnae have to come further. Ye are right about the weather, and mayhap a respite here overnight may show clear skies tomorrow."

Hew's face creased with relief. "I'll see if the innkeeper has a spare room for ye, then. And a warm meal wouldnae go amiss, either." He gave the horse a pat and shuffled across the yard toward the welcoming glow of the inn.

Marsaili ducked her head. She hated misleading faithful Hew. She shied from calling it lying, though there was scarcely a difference between agreeing with him then leaving on her own as soon as he was out of sight, and arguing the fact she dare not linger. It had been wrong to allow Hew to accompany her this far to begin with, but he and his wife, Flore, had been with her since her birth, and though Flore lay dead many miles south and nearly a year gone, Hew maintained his position of self-proclaimed body guard and chief worrier in her life. But his old bones needed rest and warmth much more than hers did, and if she wanted to grow old, she must keep moving.

"I'd fancy a rare spring day, myself," she told the horse. It flicked an ear and pawed the earth, sending up chunks of packed snow from beneath its hoof. Marsaili eyed the ground in the yard, surprised to find little trace of mud or stone beneath the gathering snow.

She bit a chapped lip and tightened her cloak about her, pulling at the strings. Retrieving a pair of fur-lined leather gloves from the small bag at her side, she slipped them over stiff fingers.

"We'd best be away before Hew comes looking for us. In this weather, he willnae follow us. He'll be praying we'll come to our senses and return." She peered at the path leading from the inn to the road some distance away. A vague dip in the snow indicated where the trail lay, with no indication of what hid beneath the cold white surface.

No, I won't be coming back. A chill skittered down her spine that had nothing to do with the cold and everything to do with the man who almost certainly hunted her even in the worsening storm.

CHAPTER TWO

T HE CART STUTTERED to a halt. Geoffrey relaxed his death-grip on the sides of the conveyance and blew out a sigh of relief.

Thank the Lord for small favors! I swear I'd rather walk than spend one more moment in this torture chamber.

He grabbed his cane and stretched toward the door which opened magically to a man covered in white.

"Good Lord, Wythevede!" Geoffrey exclaimed, noting the snow crusted to the man's cloak and the blast of frigid air that leapt inside the conveyance. "Is it that bad outside?"

The man's eyes watered and crystals sparkled on the tips of his lashes as he blinked. The tip of his nose glowed bright red, but a fine line of blue about his lips alarmed Geoffrey. He scooted aside and motioned for the man to climb into the meager warmth of the cart. Wythevede gave him a startled look and shook his head.

"Thank ye kindly, M'lord, but 'tis not my place. However, the men have secured a small hut with a shed of sorts for the horses." He gave a long-suffering sigh. "Though the place looks as if it hasn't been lived in for years and is certainly not worthy of you, M'lord."

Geoffrey ignored the man's pandering. He was becoming accustomed to it and so far it had gained him excellent lodgings at inns along their journey, and cost him nothing more than the occasional quelling glance. Which he hardly needed to practice and rarely noticed when he used it.

"Beggars cannot be choosers, Wythevede," he chided gently. "I am thankful we have shelter and are not forced to wait the storm out in the open." He again gathered his cane to his side and heaved himself to his feet, stooping low to clear the door's opening. Biting air licked eagerly at his skin as he exited the cart, and he gripped the cart's frame, careful not to slip on the icy ground as his feet sought purchase. He shrugged his cape close to his neck, denying access to the dancing flakes of snow and ice that obscured much of the surroundings.

"I had no intention of traveling if the weather

turned this bad," he commented, the wind whisking his words away from the often rather deaf ears of his driver. Wythevede hunched beneath his wool coat without any sign he'd heard Lord de Wylde. He trudged to the head of the team where he grasped the lead horse's bridle and led the pair into a ramshackle building not far from the cottage.

A heavily cloaked man stepped through the door-way and gave Geoffrey a nod. "There was a supply of wood already in the house and Walter has started a fire to warm you, Saint." He gave Geoffrey a quick survey. "Is there anything you need other than your bag from the cart?"

Geoffrey stifled the twinge of annoyance of having his oldest friend see the need to care for him like an invalid. Though he had done so once before—for several months—and it was difficult to fault Simon for his continued diligence and care. He forced a slight smile.

"See that Wythevede doesn't freeze solid out here. His lips are turning an interesting shade of blue."

Simon gave a short nod and trudged through the snow to the shed. Geoffrey leaned heavily on his cane as he made his way cautiously up the walkway. The door swung easily open at his touch and he was relieved to feel the feeble heat from the tiny hearth as he stepped inside.

"Have a care for the draft," Walter barked, not sparing Geoffrey a look over his shoulder from where he knelt before the hearth, coddling the small flame. "A small sneeze would put out the fire. The wood is dry but so old it is crumbling rather than burning." He sat back on his heels, dusting his hands on his thighs. "That should do until I can search out something better. Mayhap the furniture can be appropriated. Seems the best use for the lot."

Geoffrey glanced about, noting a heavy table, two chairs, a stool with three legs—though it appeared to have once boasted four—and a bed in the corner of the single room, its pile of blankets an indeterminate shade of dirt.

"Try the mattress. Whatever it is stuffed with, 'tis straw now. Then use whatever you must. 'Tis damn uncomfortable weather to be without a fire."

He hobbled across the dirt floor, bare of rushes or cover of any sort. Stretching his hands toward the small flame, he waited for the warmth to chase away the stabbing ache in his leg that had begun the moment he'd exited the closed cart. The pain dulled slightly and he breathed a sigh of relief.

"I'll have Wythevede warm a stone to help with the pain," Walter said. "Once the wagon is unloaded, we'll sort something out to eat."

"A mug of mulled wine from the case in the back of the wagon would be welcome."

Walter cracked a half-grin. "And ruin your reputation, Saint?"

"For the purpose of saving lives, my son," Geoffrey intoned in a moderate voice. "Which has always been wine's first objective. It says so in the Bible." He glanced away. "Though that is no longer my concern."

With a nod of understanding, Walter strode to the door and disappeared into the rising storm.

MARSAILI SWORE UNDER her breath as her gloves slipped again on the reins. A thin layer of ice coated the leather straps, making them difficult to grasp. The horse stumbled, yanking a rein from her hands. Marsaili leaned forward, grabbing for the leather, but her mount planted a hoof squarely on the dangling rein, jerking his head upward at the ensuing tug on his mouth. The hard knot at the top of his head smacked Marsaili squarely on the nose, and her vision swam with tears as she covered her face with a hand against the pain.

"King Henry and a strumpet!" she yelped as blood ran down her chin. Still fighting the hold of the rein, her horse backed a step, tossing his head up and down. Off-balance, Marsaili grabbed at his mane, but the wiry strands slipped through her nearly nerveless fingers and she lurched to the side, windmilling an arm in an effort to keep her balance. She had the presence of mind to tuck her shoulder as she realized the battle lost, landing on her back in the drifted snow as she rolled, saving herself the inconvenience of a broken arm.

She raised up on her elbows, pulling in air to lungs flattened upon impact. Catching her breath, she glared at the horse who dropped his head and now stared at her as though wondering how she'd gotten from the saddle to the middle of the trail.

"Ye amadan!" Muttering darkly, she gave him a brush-off as he snuffled her face. "If I wasnae so c-c-cold, I'd . . . ." Her voice trailed off as she struggled to her feet. Though sturdy, her boots found no purchase on the slick ground and she found herself once again on her back in the snow. With a sigh of annoyance, she sat, grabbing a handful of snow to pack against her injured nose.

"Ow!" The side of her nose and her left eye were tender, protesting as she gently prodded the area. "'Twill likely be purple in the morning." Calming, she stood gingerly and dusted what she could of the matted snow from her skirts, then gathered the reins. The right leather strap dangled a few inches from the horse's bit, the longer end half-buried in the snow.

"Och, that is wonderful." She eyed the horse. "Ye had to break it, didn't ye? How am I to guide ye?" Frowning, she glanced about. "Not that we can go much further. I'd forgotten what a good snow looks like." She shivered. "Or feels like."

Wet flakes of snow as big as her hand flurried about her, carried on the rising wind. The only sound was the soughing of the trees and the creak of burdened branches. The bottom fell out of Marsaili's stomach as she realized how alone she was.

She gripped the horse's rein tighter. "I'm not even sure which way is north, anymore." She glanced at the ground. "And I'm not sure where the road is, either."

The horse snorted and shoved her with the flat of his bony forehead. Marsaili stumbled a step forward. "I dinnae for a moment believe ye know what ye're talking about," she informed the horse, lifting her head to keep her courage up. "Ye cannae tell north from south. Ye are an English beast, after all."

So maligning the poor horse for his country of origin, she touched the tip of her nose lightly. Wiggling it gently did not begin the bleeding anew, and she determined the wound survivable.

A blast of wind flattened her snow-damp skirts about her legs and she shivered at the unwelcome contact. Taking a deep breath, she wondered where she could possibly shelter until the storm blew itself out. To her surprise, she discovered the hint of smoke in the heavy, damp air.

The day, though only hours old, was giving up its light to the onslaught of the storm, and Marsaili peered intently at the tree line, searching for a hint of smoke to guide her to a place of refuge.

There! A thin, pale gray line of smoke rose lazily against the leaden sky a moment before a gust of wind swept it away. She tugged on the horse's bridle. "Come on! Mayhap I can find ye a bit of hay to fill yer belly. If ye are silent as a mouse, whoever lives there willnae notice."

The horse nudged her again, his bony head flat against her back.

"Dinnae think ye can talk me into a bag of oats, laddie. 'Tis something people *do* notice."

For some reason, the bulk of the horse's head pressed against her gave Marsaili a bit of comfort, and she continued to speak to him as though he understood her words. If it gave her a bit of confidence and helped take her mind off the soul-numbing storm, she was willing to continue in this vein, though the cold stiffened the muscles of her jaw and distorted her words.

"Ye know I'll have to gi' ye a name since it looks as if we'll spend th' night together. No' an English one, though I suppose yer ma'd roll over in her grave to hear ye sporting a Scottish moniker. I think I'll call ye *Hew*. I do miss the auld man, though he worries enough for a dozen auld women. 'Tis comforting to speak as though he's still with me."

The horse had no answer, and plodded slowly along behind her. Marsaili halted at the edge of a small clearing, staring longingly at the smoke lowering over the roof of the house as it chased the flakes of snow. Her gaze found a low shed, the wheel of a wagon protruding from the opening of the roofed lean-to.

She carefully inspected the ground at the doorway to the shed, as well as the space between it and the house. The snow blew in dense white clouds, obscuring any trace of footprints, assuring her the inhabitants of the cottage were well-ensconced within.

"I believe yon is our bower for the night." She gave the cottage a wistful look, then squared her shoulders. "Let us inspect our lodging," she whispered. Taking up the newly-dubbed Hew's rein, she made her way carefully across the open area to the shed, ears alert for shouts of warning.

"If we were in Scotland, I'd not worry about my welcome," she grumbled. "Bluidy English are a suspicious lot. Of a certainty, the fewer who know I've been here, the better off we both shall be." She glanced over her shoulder as a sudden sense of warning blossomed between her shoulder blades.

Nothing moved in the silent forest behind her, and the swath she and Hew cut through the snow vanished beneath the continued snowfall as though it had never existed.

CHAPTER THREE

G EOFFREY STIFLED A **groan**. No matter how accustomed he should be to the effect cold had on his thigh, there was a limit to his tolerance. With no choice but to haul himself to his feet and walk, forcing warming blood into his injured leg, he grabbed for his cane and rose slowly to his feet.

"Anything you need, Saint?" Walter murmured from his position near the door. Damp spots on the floor attested to his recent foray outside as he kept watch, as no windows graced the hovel.

"Nay. Keep your seat. My leg is bothersome, but nothing a brisk walk will not help."

Geoffrey winced at Walter's skeptical look, eyes narrowed at the thought of Geoffrey attempting anything other than a creeping pace. He scowled and turned away, keeping the thump of his cane to soft levels to avoid waking the others.

The muscles in his thigh eased after numerous laps

across the hardened dirt floor. Walter shoved away from his stance at the door and crossed to one of the sleeping forms.

"Wake up, Wythevede," he grunted, giving the man a shove with his booted foot. "The wind died down an hour or more ago, and we need to check on the horses."

The elderly man groaned as he sat upright, dragging a hand through his ragged hair, making it stand comically on end. He gave the knight a glare but rose without further argument. Stomping his feet into his boots, he dragged his cloak over his shoulders and jammed his knitted cap over his pate. Shuffling through the door Walter held open, he and the knight slipped into the cold dawn.

Simon rose as well, striding to the hearth to prod the fire. He tossed a couple of small logs into the resulting blaze and Geoffrey limped near, drawn to the heat. Reaching for the pot of water resting on the hearth, he hoisted it to the iron bar over the fire.

"Here, Milord. I will fix something to warm our bellies," Simon offered as he reached for their pack of supplies. He inclined his head in apology. "You are not an invalid, Saint. Nor are you incapable. I am here to see to your comfort. 'Tis my job as it has ever been."

"We three used to share alike," Geoffrey murmured, lowering himself gingerly to the rough stone of the raised hearth.

"That time has passed, Milord," Simon replied. "Yet you were always our leader, even as lads and later in battle. We must always adapt to our changing circumstances." His lips curved gently upward, though his eyes saddened. "Your knighthood for a priesthood, now exchanged for a lordship."

"A lordship I do not want."

"You have no control over your brothers' fates. No one would have wished them an early death, but the title now falls to you."

Geoffrey nodded, bleakness stealing over his soul. "My duty is clear. I know this in my head. But my heart will miss them."

"Even their pranks?" Simon asked, his smile broadening.

The question prodded a grunt from Geoffrey. "Their pranks as lads became well-known exploits on and off the battlefield. I'd be remiss if I thought they would be missed by everyone."

"Mayhap a few young ladies shed some tears, and

knights will now have to seek others of similar prowess to fight. Though the Lord knows where they will find them."

The cottage door flew open forestalling the contemplation of the plight of warring knights. Wythevede leapt into the room amid a blast of frigid air, his eyes wide with alarm.

"There's a dead woman in the barn!"

Simon and Geoffrey startled at the news and Simon rushed to the door. Geoffrey hobbled in Simon's wake across the room as Walter burst through, the limp body of a young woman in his arms. He strode directly to the hearth, clumps of snow falling from his boots as he tracked across the floor.

"Push another log on the fire," he directed as he sat on the hearth, all but shoving the woman atop the blaze.

"Have a care for the flames, Walter," Geoffrey murmured. He leaned over the woman, noting the smooth skin of her face—a faint lavender hue that would look better as a spring mantle than a skin tone. He gently swept tangled copper-red hair from her brow.

"She's young," he said, smoothing a hand over her

icy cheek.

"She's the *wallydraigle* from the inn!" Wythevede exclaimed, standing on his toes to peer over Geoffrey's shoulder.

Geoffrey swung about, the warning light in his eyes immediately silencing the old man and setting him rocking back on his heels. "This woman is neither worthless nor slovenly. 'Tis travel that has stained her clothing—which is of fine quality, though you haven't noticed. And none of God's children are worthless. It would behoove you to remember that, Wythevede."

Abandoning the set-down, he returned to the young woman who hung lifeless in Walter's arms. He lifted a closed eyelid, noting the resilient texture of the orb within. "She may yet live."

Walter gave him a startled gaze. "I'd felt no pulse."

Geoffrey grunted as he reached for the knife at his belt and sliced the wet strings fastening the woman's cloak. "Yet you tried to warm her."

"I had to try," the knight admitted.

"Of course. 'Twas the right thing to do." Geoffrey nodded. "And God may reward us for your care today."

He stripped the cloak away, letting it fall to the

floor, then attended to her gown in a similar manner, slicing through the heavy, soaked fabric rather than bother with the swollen ties of her lacings. To his surprise, his hands encountered the tell-tale lump of a sheath at her right thigh, as well as one attached to the back of the bodice of her under gown. With some misgivings, he left the daggers in place, knowing he would be alert to any furtive movements she might make. If she lived.

Determining the under gown would not impede the warming process much, he left it on her as well, allowing the small bit of modesty it would afford her.

"Hang her cloak to dry and fetch my blanket," he barked at Wythevede, giving the man a withering stare for his gap-mouthed gawk at the nearly naked woman. Chastened, the man averted his gaze and grabbed the indicated garment from the floor, ignoring the ruined gown. He tossed the cloak over the back of a chair and quickly returned with Lord de Wylde's blanket.

Transferred from Walter's arms, the woman disappeared within the folds of Geoffrey's cloak, not even so much as the top of her head visible. Simon dragged a chair before the hearth and Geoffrey settled on its seat, opening the edges of his cloak to admit the heat of the fire within. He accepted the blanket and carefully wrapped the woman before returning her to the potentially life-saving spot beneath his coat, against his rapidly beating heart.

>>><<<

THOUSANDS OF NEEDLES prickled her fingers and toes. Marsaili twitched, tried to kick, clenched and un-clenched her fists. Anything to halt the terrible sensation. Nothing worked. Pain crept up her limbs and she whimpered. Someone smoothed her cheek and murmured in her ear.

"Easy, Milady. You nearly froze to death. Welcome back."

"Hurts," she whimpered, eyes tightly closed. She wanted nothing more than to fall back into the nothingness where the pain did not exist.

"Aye. But that means you are warming. 'Twill soon pass."

Marsaili groaned as someone shoved against her back, forcing her to a seated position.

"Drink this," the voice commanded. "'Twill warm your insides."

The idea of being warm again was enticing, but it

was too much effort to open her mouth and accept the contents of the mug beneath her nose. The aroma tempted, however, and she reluctantly lifted eyelids that unbelievably seemed to weigh a pound or more each. She blinked, trying to determine where she was, for her last memory was of sheltering in a stable between the furry forms of two well-muscled horses.

Why had she been in a barn, for the love of St. Andrew? She blinked furiously, as though the exercise could fan her brain to life. Memories, unconnected, flashed before her. People in mourning? Fear. Outrage. A horse named Hew. No, that was incorrect. Hew had been her servant these past years, he and his wife. Sadness—Hew's wife, her nurse since birth, was gone. Another face. Edmund—a sneer, evil triumph.

Marsaili shook her head as panic overwhelmed her. Had Edmund caught her? Who offered her the drink? Poison?

She jerked back with a cry, unable to move her arms, captured, trussed, incapable of escape—

"Cease!" the man commanded, gripping her firmly. "You are in no danger. Give yourself a moment to regain your composure. Walter will care for you."

She felt herself being passed into another's arms.

They bundled her gently, and, exhausted, Marsaili fell through wakefulness into a deep sleep.

WARMTH. SHE'D NEVER been so warm. Marsaili sighed. It felt absolutely wonderful. She opened her eyes, taking a moment to adjust to the low light. Red and yellow flames danced on a hearth, giving her the reason for the heat seeping into her bones. Undulating shadows mated in a leisurely fashion on the wall, and she noted dark lumps scattered on the floor at her feet.

Bodies? She instinctively tried to pull her feet up, away from the carnage, but her movements were hindered and she discovered a heavy blanket swaddled her head to toe.

One of the nondescript mounds groaned and rolled over and Marsaili swallowed a trickle of hysterical laughter that threatened to spill from her throat.

Men. Sleeping. Abruptly the cobwebs cleared from her mind and she sat upright, shucking the blanket away with rapid flicks of her hands. A blast of chill air struck her skin and she realized she wore nothing more than her thin under dress beneath the blanket. She drew her knees up to her chest and clutched the blanket about her shoulders. The chair beneath her gave a warning creak.

"'Tis good to see you awake, Milady."

She whipped her head around, wincing as a band of pain tightened around her head at the sudden motion. Placing cautious fingertips to her temple, she could find no reason for the sensation, but her head throbbed just the same.

A dark-haired man stared at her, his gaze assessing. Marsaili drew back slightly, discomfited by the close scrutiny. He touched her head, slid the back of a hand across her brow, cupped her chin in his palm.

"Would ye care to count my teeth?" she growled, ill at ease with his attention.

One corner of the man's mouth gave the tiniest jerk, but failed to become a smile. His eyes remained placid as he sat on the edge of the hearth and dropped his hands to his lap.

"You appear to be recovering nicely," he noted. "Tell me what you were doing in our barn last night."

Marsaili bristled at his command, though it was spoken gently enough. "Sleeping," she replied. He continued to gaze at her and she bit her lip. "Freezing."

The man sighed. "You have nothing to fear from

me. I can perhaps be of some help, however, if you confide in me."

He tilted his head, the glow from the fire casting golden tones on his skin, chiseling his features in shadows. Something clicked in Marsaili's head. *Of course! He is the man from the inn.* Her eyes narrowed speculatively. *He* did *champion me. Or, rather, my cause.*

"My servant dinnae accompany me beyond the inn," she admitted, "and when the storm became too severe to continue, I was forced to find shelter. I dinnae know 'twas yer stable." She peered at him from beneath her lashes, daring him to find fault with her tale.

"You rode out alone?" A heavy, dark eyebrow surged upward and his lips thinned with displeasure. "Do you not utilize what wit the Lord has given you? There are reasons beyond mere social convention for a woman to not travel unchaperoned."

Marsaili scowled. "Dinnae concern yerself with me, Sir. I can take care of myself."

"Two sentences more incorrect I vow I've not heard in many days. You are now my concern, precisely *because* you cannot fend for yourself."

Marsaili opened her mouth to deliver a blistering

set-down, but shut it abruptly as another man approached. His shaggy brown hair appeared to have seen little of a comb in the past few days, but his eyes rounded with kindness and concern.

"Are you better, Milady?" he asked.

"He and my man, Wythevede, found you in the stable," the first man said. "You may state your gratitude and your name to Sir Walter de Ellerton."

Marsaili lifted her chin. "My thanks to ye, Sir Walter."

"Your name?" the first man prompted when she did not continue.

"You may call me Marsaili," she replied stiffly.

"Just Marsaili? Nothing else?"

"To a man I've yet to meet?" She tossed a hostile look at the dark-haired man. "Marsaili is sufficient."

"I beg your pardon for my omission, Milady. I am Lord de Wylde." He executed a small bow from the waist, not bothering to stand.

Marsaili arched a brow. "Are ye always stuffy, Lord de Wylde?" she drawled.

"He's always *right*," a third man said as he crossed the room to join them. "'Tis why we call him *The Saint*."

Marsaili's mouth clapped shut, jarring her teeth. A shiver slid through her belly. She worked her jaw to loosen it. She'd heard of The Saint, and the stories were enough to frighten grown men.

"I thought ye needed a couple of miracles and an exemplary life to attain sainthood," she ventured.

"Postmortem miracles are required, alas, and Milord is very much still alive," the third man quipped, a twinkle in his eye.

"And it seems an exemplary life has yet to come to pass," Lord de Wylde added.

"'Twas said after ye killed a thousand men, ye retreated to a monastery to prepare yer soul," Marsaili whispered.

"Hardly a true account," the other man said. His golden, shorn locks curled about his head, making him the better candidate for the appearance of a saint—or perhaps an angel. "My name is Sir Simon de Bretteby. I believe we met at the inn."

CHAPTER FOUR

O F COURSE. HOW could she forget? Marsaili had been desperate for a new mount, heart-sore to leave her own horse behind, angry at the stable man's inability to look past her sex and simply offer her a new beast. And she'd been rude. Quite rude, in fact.

"I hope you understand I wasnae angry with ye, Sir Simon," she said, gentling her voice in apology. "The stable master was not in an accommodating mood, and it tweaked my ire to have my wishes belittled." She tilted her head and gave a winsome smile. "I dinnae mean to insult ye—personally."

"I have dismissed the matter from my mind," Simon avowed. "The man had earned your animosity, and though we were late leaving the inn, I was not against watching him receive his due from a lady such as you."

Lord de Wylde cleared his throat. "If I may inter-rupt this mutual admiration faire, I would like to question milady a bit more, her actions of yesterday notwithstanding." He gave Simon a jerk of his chin. "I believe we could all use something warm in our bellies, if you would be so kind."

Simon ducked his head in answer and set about rummaging through a pack on the floor. Marsaili gave her attention to Geoffrey.

"What do ye wish from me?" she asked warily. She would dearly love a warm meal before she left, but she owed the man no answers as to her conduct—now or the day before. If such was the price of her food, well, she'd face the day on an empty stomach.

"First, let us attend you." He motioned for her to stand. "Have you any injuries beyond those suffered from the night in the barn?"

Marsaili snugged the blanket closer. "Nae. I've no injuries." Her gaze narrowed. "And I'd like my gown back, if ye please." Her icy tone told the meddling Lord de Wylde what she thought of a man who'd divest a lady of her clothing without her permission.

"That is not possible," he replied with a nonchalance that irritated Marsaili further.

"What do ye mean, *not possible*? What have ye done with my clothes?"

"Your gown was saturated and the lacings impossible to undo. I simply cut your gown away as it was more important to warm you than worry about what happened to your clothes."

"Ye WHAT?" Her shriek drew the two knights immediately to her side, and the door to the hut banged open.

"Close the door!" Geoffrey barked. Wythevede slammed the wooden panel shut, forcing it to latch as it rebounded on its creaking leather hinges. "And remove yer cap in the presence of a lady."

The old man's eyes bugged at the unwarranted reprimand, but tugged the offending hat from his head, banging the wool on his thigh to remove the dusting of snow. He leaned close to Walter. "Is the wench truly a lady?" he whispered.

Walter spared him a glance, but did not bother to confirm Geoffrey's statement.

"I want my gown—now!" Marsaili demanded, slipping to her feet onto the bare floor. She hopped lightly from one foot to the other, disliking the touch of cold earth on her bare soles. "And my boots—and stockings—and, oh!" She fumbled for words, incensed at her handling at the hands of the English lord.

"Wythevede, bring Lady Marsaili needle and thread and her gown."

Marsaili stared in disbelief at the dress the old man handed her. Its front was cleaved in twain from the neckline to the waist, rendering it easily removed, though impossible to mend without a jagged seam. She snagged the small mending bag and set about sewing a seam to close the gaping flaw. Sending Lord de Wylde a murderous glare for his part in her struggles, she settled back in her chair and bent to her work.

Geoffrey jerked a shoulder. *Ungrateful wench. I will be glad to send her on her way. Her defiance disrupts the calm life I have garnered for myself these past months.*

His conscience nudged him as he watched her wiggle her bottom to a more comfortable position in her chair. The blanket hid what his arms had held during the long day as he'd waited for her to awaken, his heart thudding ominously each time her breathing slowed. But he remembered every moment—and every curve.

She should not travel alone. It would be wrong to allow her to leave us unprotected. His decision was easily made. She would travel with them when they resumed their journey.

Simon handed him a bowl of porridge and a steaming mug of mulled wine. He accepted both with a nod of thanks. "Give milady the same, though water her wine,"

Marsaili's head jerked up and she sent a narrowed gaze to Simon. "Ye willnae water my wine."

"You need a clear head," Geoffrey told her. "Ladies drink watered wine."

She laughed, and at the soft, sensual sound, Geoffrey forgot to be annoyed with her. "I dinnae know where ye get yer information about ladies and their drink preferences, but I also enjoy a glass of whisky of an evening."

"No lady I know drinks to excess," Geoffrey said, his voice lowering in warning. The young woman ignored his tone and leveled a slender finger in his direction.

"Och, the ladies *ye* know—and I ask if *lady* is the proper term—are the women who follow the armies and likely have a need to drink themselves senseless from time to time. Have a care ye dinnae place me in their category." She returned to her mending, gripping her lower lip between her small white teeth as she placed each tiny stitch.

Shocked at her set-down, he reconsidered his original plan. *She can learn to lie in the bed of her own making and see to her own safety. I did not ask to play nursemaid to an opinionated woman who does not know her place.*

Simon set a bowl and mug before Marsaili on the hearth. "Thank ye, sir knight," she warbled, full of warmth and kindness for the man.

The man who does her bidding. Geoffrey scowled and scooped porridge into his mouth, washing it down with the mulled wine. *'Twill not be me.*

Marsaili set her mending aside and picked up her food, sniffing the wine appreciatively.

"A lovely combination of spices," she approved. Taking a sip, she held the liquid in her mouth for a moment before swallowing. "Quite nice." She grinned at Simon. "And warm. Blessedly warm."

"We found you in the stable in a pile of straw," Walter said, accepting his repast from Simon. "Did you not wish to chance your reception in the cottage rather than risk your death in the barn?"

Marsaili's demeanor became cautious, though a slight smile lingered on her lips. "A woman traveling alone? Risk who knows what from strangers who could be less than dishonorable?" She slanted a look to Geoffrey. "I bedded down between the two horses pulling yer wagon and 'twas quite warm for a while. But it dinnae last. 'Twas shelter, but not enough."

"Enough to keep you alive, though barely," Walter noted with a nod. "But 'tis a good thing you arrived here and not at some rogues' gathering. The Saint will not let harm befall you." He indicated himself and Simon with a wave of his mug. "Nor will we."

"'Tis good to know, Sir. Though I am afraid I will soon be on my way. Your company has been appreciated, as are your efforts on my behalf." Again she cut a glance at Geoffrey, setting his teeth on edge. "But I am sure our paths are separate ones."

"You will ride with us," Geoffrey informed her, changing his mind once again. Simon and Walter gave him startled looks and his neck warmed. "The Church teaches us to care for women and children," he reminded them. He returned Marsaili's furious stare. "*And* those unable to fend for themselves. 'Tis not safe for you to travel alone, and you will be under our protection until your journey ends or you are passed on to another for safe-keeping."

"Here's a *miracle* for yer impending sainthood,

Lord de Wylde! 'Tis a *miracle* no one has kilt ye out of a fit of total aggravation for yer interfering ways. I told ye I dinnae need yer care, and I meant it!"

"I heard you, and you do," Geoffrey intoned evenly, reining in his building annoyance with supreme effort. Never had anyone—much less a woman—gainsaid him as this woman did. "I am used to having my orders followed to the letter, so let me speak plainly. You will ride with us until we reach my estate at Galewood, which is not far from the Scottish border. At that time, escort will be arranged for you that will take you to your destination. No other options, opinions or attempts to sway a change in my order will be entertained."

He paused, waiting for the woman to explode. Her cheeks flamed, her neck arched, and sparks flew from her clear blue eyes. *Impressive!* The only drawback was the thinning of her full lips, marring their lush perfection. And, of course, 'twas now likely she had a full arsenal of vindictive words ready to hurl at him.

"Do I make myself clear?" he asked, forestalling her tirade.

"Ye amadan!" she hissed. "Ye dinnae care what damage ye cause. I have reason to not ride with ye, or any man. I willnae have my journey impeded by such as ye."

"Such as me?" he returned, curious as to what specific fault she found with him.

She waved an arm in the air, encompassing everyone in the room. "Ye have two horses where four would give better service pulling that wagon. Yer driver is elderly and likely not capable of demanding the best of what nags he has. And two men are an impressively small guard for a landed English lord." She cast a look at their booted feet. "And, 'twere it not for the gold spurs ye wear, I'd find myself wondering at their abilities."

Stung, Walter rose to his full height. "The three of us are completely formidable, milady," he informed her, his voice rising with each word.

"Everyone knows the might of The Wolfe rides at our back," Simon added with a nonchalant shrug. "It has been quite some time since anyone was foolish enough to challenge us."

Marsaili drew back, a chill coursing up her spine at the thought of these men aligned with the formidable baron, Lord William de Wolfe, the king's champion.

She suppressed a shudder. "Nevertheless, there are

but two of ye now, unless milord fights from his chair. Though he has a commanding presence, I have yet to see him without his cane."

"Despite our grievous faults, the fact remains you are safer with us than without us," Geoffrey clipped. "Make yourself presentable and begin your sojourn with our lackluster party by helping with a few of the chores. We will bide the night here and leave at first light."

Marsaili swept her gown into her arms, brandishing the needle as she would a sword. "I will finish my mending and take my leave, Milord. Sleeping the evening and night away is a luxury I can ill afford."

"Upon my word, she is not to leave the cottage," Geoffrey commanded, feeling a vein in his forehead throb.

Mutiny fouling her brow, Marsaili bent to her work, her needle flying in and out of the fabric. She bit the thread below the knot and turned the gown over in her lap to address the laces.

A tear fell from her cheek, a dark spot marking the green hue of the bodice. Geoffrey rose and limped to her side. Placing his fingers lightly over her small hand, he stilled the furious pluck at the tangled strings.

"Pardon, Milady, but I do not perceive why you do not wish our protection. I admit I have always known and valued the security being the nephew of Lord William de Wolfe affords. Mayhap you have never realized the luxury of certain safety?"

Marsaili sniffed and made a quick swipe at her cheek with the back of a hand. Geoffrey's voice softened. "What, besides your pique at me, causes you such distress? We swear to protect you, and yet it angers you?"

His heart tripped in his chest as she lifted her watery gaze to his. Her skin glowed in the firelight, but only the flames lent color to her thin, pale cheeks. Gone was the defiance, the anger, the contempt. In the depths of her eyes, he saw only fear.

She made no further effort to wipe the tears that tumbled down her face. "Ye amadan," she whispered, "For all of yer posturing and telling me what is right or wrong, ere this is over, ye will have likely cost me my life."

CHAPTER FIVE

T HE CREAK OF the enclosed wagon ground out a cadence behind them.

Plod, plod, creak, jangle. Plod, plod, creak, jangle.

Marsaili shrank deeper into the hood of her cloak. Sunlight sparkled on the snow, trees, and ground alike as though covered in the costliest white silk and encrusted with diamonds. But the sun's warmth and brilliance did not find its way into Marsaili's heart.

Damn, damn, damn! 'Twould have been simpler had I succumbed to the cold. At this slow pace, 'tis only a matter of time before Edmund's men catch up with me.

Every rustle in the forest, every crack of an over-loaded branch caused her to jump in her saddle, sending her mount sideways to bump against one or the other destriers Walter and Simon rode on either side of her. With such heavily muscled horseflesh and mounted armored knights at her side, she should have felt safe. Instead, she felt trapped.

Plod, plod, creak, jangle. Plod, plod, creak, jangle.

She cringed and tugged the tip of her hood lower. *The noise it makes could alert scoundrels all the way to Lancaster!*

"Do you not enjoy the sunlight, Lady Marsaili?" Walter asked. His concern seemed most sincere. Did he assume a proprietary interest since he had been the one to find her in the barn? Marsaili stole a look at him from within her cowl. His shaggy brown hair was covered by his helmet, which also hid his rather long nose. Though she wondered if his habit of staring down its length over-emphasized its size. He was quite tall, and she remembered him as lean beneath the bulk of his armor. Dark eyes sparkled through the visor.

"I am cautious, 'tis all," she said. "What if we meet with scoundrels?"

Simon laughed aloud, the merry sound sending a startled bird to flight. "You were hardly worried about being noticed at the inn or when you took shelter with our horses." He rested a gloved hand on his armored thigh. "Whom do you fear, Milady? Tell us that we might better protect you."

Marsaili scowled and tilted her chin up. "I am

merely going home and wish to be about it as quickly as possible."

"Where is home?" Walter asked.

Her head swiveled to the knight. "Across the border."

"Your accent is clearly Scottish, but I detect an English influence. Could you have lived among us for a time?"

Damn them for their interfering interest. I dinnae wish to spend my time gabbing when I should be planning my escape.

"A wee time, mayhap," she allowed, the incline of her head not inviting further questions.

Simon took up the challenge. "Have you kin in England, then?"

Marsaili sat straight-backed on her horse and did not answer.

"You are of an age to be married," Simon needled. "Or mayhap you tended a family member who lives in England rather than marry. Why did you not wed?"

Marsaili fumed silently, not bothering to send the knight the glare he so richly deserved as she could not appreciate his expression behind his visor. She kicked her mount to a slightly faster pace instead.

"Don't pick on the lady, Simon," Walter grunted. "'Tis not chivalrous."

"And The Saint would not be pleased?" Simon's helmeted head bent forward as though in apology. "I but jest with Milady in an attempt to pass the day. And mayhap learn a bit about this lovely lady whose life you saved."

"I think she's a runaway," Wythevede shouted from his perch atop the wagon. "I don't know why we're bothering with the likes of her."

Marsaili gasped and pivoted in her saddle, pinning the elderly man with a stare. "Not that I answer to ye, but my business is my own. If ye dinnae wish to consort with the likes of me, might I suggest ye simply abandon me to my wishes? I scarcely see how a wizened auld man can be of benefit to me."

"Wizened?" he screeched, rising to a half-crouch from his seat. "Fine words coming from a *wallydraigle* such as yourself!"

The wagon jostled violently as a wheel slid over a rock partially submerged in the snow. Wythevede gave a cry as he clawed at the wooden seat for his balance. He sawed at the reins, hauling the team to a stop. The door to the wagon banged open and Lord de Wylde's head appeared, the scowl on his face signaling his displeasure.

"Have I not warned you about the use of that word, Wythevede?" he growled. "Engaging in name-calling cost your attention to duty and tossed me about in this wretched box. Again."

His gaze slid from the sufficiently cowed driver to the trio seated silently upon their horses. "Milady, join me in the wagon."

Marsaili sent him a startled look. "I willnae subject myself to that particular torture, thank ye just the same. I am quite comfortable on my horse."

"You appear cold, despite the sunny day, and have retreated into your cloak for warmth. I would be remiss if I did not offer you the meager warmth of the wagon. And you are perilously close to becoming the center of a most embarrassing situation."

Geoffrey waited as Marsaili shifted in her saddle, obviously unwilling to cede her position to join him. But he was interested to note she caught his implication without him having to spell out the consequences should she continue to defy him. Though he questioned the sanity of his decision to bring her inside the wagon where her presence would inconvenience him much more than mere thoughts of her already did, the brouhaha he'd just witnessed as his driver's attention wavered, proved the need.

Drumming his fingertips on the doorframe, he peered at the sky. "'Twill only become colder from this point on. Tie her nag to the rear of the wagon, Simon. Walter, help her dismount."

"I can get down by myself," she fumed, snatching her hands away as Walter reached up for her. She swung a leg over the horse's back, landing with a bit of a totter on the ground. She clutched the horse's tack for balance, then picked up the front of her skirts and stalked to the wagon, sweeping a swath through the snow. Geoffrey offered his hand, but she grasped both sides of the door frame and hauled herself inside.

"'Tis cold in here, too," she grumbled, taking the bench across from him. "At least I was getting exercise outside."

"Sit over here, if you please." Geoffrey motioned to a spot beside him as he sank onto the thick cushions and pile of sumptuous furs on his seat, which were notably absent on the opposite side. "I will share my furs and what little heat remains in the stone Wythevede heated for me this morning."

Marsaili shrugged, irritation eloquent in the pout of her lips and the wrinkles marring her brow. "I am fine where I am."

"And choose to cut off your nose to spite your face. Milady, it pains me to find you continue to question my honor. Have we acted with anything less than courtesy to you?" He held up a hand as she jerked upright, her mouth open to remind him of his faults. "Other than removing your gown whilst you were unconscious—which saved your life. And I left your under-gown on to assuage your modesty in the rather unlikely event you survived your night in the cold—as well as an interesting array of weapons I am happy to note you have not chosen to wield. And let us not rehash the fact I have forced you to ride with us, forestalling a forced attack on your person in the very likely event you fell afoul of brigands and scoundrels during your journey, should you continue on your own."

The woman closed her mouth and sat back on the bench, averting her head and refusing to answer.

"You will take quite a pounding over there, but suit yourself. My offer remains should you find your nether person sufficiently bruised and wish to change your mind."

Her gaze slowly slid to his. "Allowing me to choose for myself, Milord?" she drawled. "How kind of ye to consider I may hold an opinion separate from yers. I do occasionally have a mind of my own and appreciate when given the chance to exercise it."

Geoffrey knew he shouldn't needle the woman, but she did open the door herself. "Milady, so far in our brief acquaintance I've observed you arguing with a stable man over the rental of a horse and rescued you from freezing to death. My first impression was of a young woman too accustomed to getting her own way, the other of a woman who needs someone to make a few of life's more important decisions for her."

Marsaili arched fine golden eyebrows and stared down her nose at him. "Extreme circumstances, I assure ye. Though it tweaks my ire to have my wishes disregarded simply because I am a woman." She shrugged. "I dinnae make a habit of traveling in a snow storm or alone. I am merely anxious to return home."

"So you've mentioned." He braced a hand on the side of the wagon. Marsaili eyed his move with suspicion. With a grin at her startled look as Wythevede shook the team into action, he caught her before she tumbled to the floor. The wagon lurched forward then settled into a smoother mode. Tempering his amusement, Geoffrey returned Marsaili to her seat.

"And where, exactly, is home?" He continued his questions as though retrieving young women from the floor of his wagon was a not-uncommon occurrence.

"As I told the others, across the border."

"You know you'll have to do better than that. I will be unable to send an escort with you if you give me no better direction."

Her look grew cold. "Milord, meaning no disrespect, but my opinion of yer intentions, however good ye may think them, isnae verra high. Set me apace from yer company and I will find my own way home. 'Tis been a few years since I left, to be sure, but I believe the road is adequate."

"'Tis not the road I question, Milady, but the persons you will surely encounter along the way."

"Between yer noble intent and Edmund's detestable attentions, I am certain I can breeze through the Borders with little discomfiture." She tossed her head and the hood slipped back, revealing her shiny copper-red hair she'd gone to great trouble to comb and rebraid that morning, using an ivory comb from the small bag Walter had retrieved from her saddle. Her hair's fiery color seemed to warm the interior of the enclosed wagon, and the shimmer drew Geoffrey's eyes as surely as a moth to a flame. He shook off the distraction and pounced on the tiny piece of information she let slip.

"Edmund?" He hid a grin at her discomfited scowl. "Pray tell, who is Edmund?"

She pulled her cloak across her lap, staring down at it as she pleated the heavy material with her fingers.

Plod, plod, creak, jangle. Plod, plod, creak, jangle.

Geoffrey noted her pained expression at the Devil's own racket the damned conveyance relentlessly repeated as it ground along the rough North road.

After a moment, she lifted her chin and gave him a frank stare.

"Edmund is my late husband's brother."

It was Geoffrey's turn to lift a brow, astonished at the wealth of knowledge in those few words. *She is a widow, and from her tone and actions, her brother-by-marriage is not someone she cares for. In fact, she appears to place him on level with scourges, disreputable stable masters—and me.*

It was his turn to scowl. "Does he have an unnatural interest in you?" he questioned softly, realizing what he asked.

"He is the reason I am returning home, aye," she admitted, clenching her fists in her lap, the light of anger in her clear blue eyes.

Geoffrey leaned forward and placed a palm on her hands in a calming manner. "Milady, ye have naught to fear from me or my men. We would not turn you over to a man who has no legal ties to you. Please believe me. Returning you to your home is the right thing to do. We will see it through to the end."

Marsaili bit her lower lip and the gesture tugged at Geoffrey's heart. Her belligerence vanished and her mantle of self-assurance crumbled. Tears welled and Geoffrey was lost.

"I thank ye, Milord. I shouldnae involve ye in my troubles. 'Tis not my desire to entangle ye with issues not of yer making. I will confess Edmund isnae a good man." The words seemed to choke her and she swallowed hard. "He is a horrible man, capable of all manner of evil. When my husband died, Edmund took over Bellevue Castle, placing himself as lord, going through my husband's things with no care to who he offends."

"'Tis the way of things at times," Geoffrey murmured, wondering how Marsaili had changed from a woman of inconvenience to him, to one who set his protective instincts humming. "But with family close by, I do not see why you cannot return home."

She ducked her head, a gesture of avoidance Geoffrey knew well. He tipped her chin upward with a touch of his fingertips.

"Milady? You must tell me the truth. Why do you fear Edmund pursues you? If he has the lordship and all it entails, why should he care where his brother's wife resides?"

She did not answer. He stared her down.

"Edmund has always pursued me—even before Andrew died," she whispered. "I have fended him off as long as I can. But he willnae give up. He is determined to make me his wife."

CHAPTER SIX

GEOFFREY'S STOMACH CLENCHED at the thought of the lovely Marsaili forced into a marriage to such a beast. Save 'twere by the King's own edict, she should not have to endure such disgrace at the hands of her late husband's brother. As a widow and not a maidenly bargaining chip between noble houses, she deserved some choices in her life.

"He has no right to demand this?" he growled.

Marsaili startled. "I havenae been commanded to wed the brute, if that is what ye ask."

Geoffrey gave a single, determined nod. "Then we will settle this. You will not live your life in fear. Honor states he should allow you to live out your life in a dower house, unburdened by his unwelcome advances."

She eyed him narrowly. "What are ye implying, Milord?"

Geoffrey rapped on the roof of the wagon with the

head of his cane and the wagon ground to a halt. "You should not be forced to leave your home. He cannot take that away from you. I will see to it you regain all you have lost. Just now, I require a respite."

He flipped back the furs and rose to his feet, rocking unsteadily on his right leg a moment before he caught his balance.

Marsaili bounded up from her seat, clipping him on his chin, sending him tumbling back to the cushions. They slipped from the smooth wooden seat and Geoffrey toppled to the floor amid a pile of blankets and fur.

"Och, Milord! A thousand pardons!" Her hand flew to her mouth, eyes wide, aghast as she stood over him. "I only meant to say—"

Geoffrey leaned his head back and waved a hand in the air, cutting off her speech. "Enough!" Holding a palm to his chin, he worked his jaw, wincing against the pain. The door to the wagon opened and Wythevede stuck his head inside. His questioning look turned immediately to horror and he whirled about.

"Help! The woman's gone and killed Milord!"

Horses whinnied and metal clanged in a whirling melee of sound. Marsaili sank onto her bench, crouched as though ready to spring through the smallest chink in the door should Wythevede offer an opening.

"Enough!" Geoffrey lifted himself onto his elbows, furious he'd had to utter the word twice—and in the space of mere moments. He shook his head as he hauled himself to the seat.

Wythevede's wiry body was lifted away and re-placed by two helmetless heads as Walter and Simon peered inside, curiosity on their faces.

"He doesn't appear dead to me, Wythevede," Simon commented. "However, by the look on his face, I would imagine the next person to cross him will likely not live to regret his action."

Geoffrey leveled a frosty glare on his captain. "How did I come to deserve a maniacal driver and two apathetic knights?"

He grasped his cane and stepped down from the wagon, breathing in the wintry air. He tugged his cape about him, more as protection for his leg than for warmth. The crisp air was stimulating and he longed to be astride his horse, plowing through the drifted snow, the powerful muscles of his destrier between his knees. He tapped the toe of his cane against the frozen ground and forced his thoughts to the problem at hand.

"I wish a brief respite, and I would assume Milady does as well." He hobbled carefully across the icy ground, motioning Simon to attend him, leaving Walter to assist Marsaili from the wagon. They moved out of earshot and halted as Geoffrey cast a look over his shoulder.

"Milady is being chased by her late husband's brother who wishes to marry her."

Simon blinked. "That explains her pique when I asked if she'd wed," he mused.

"Did you ask her age as well?" Geoffrey bit out, a bit disturbed by his captain's insensitivity.

Simon grinned. "Nay. But I admit the question appeared to have put her nose a bit out of joint." He sobered. "I must apologize. I did not realize she was widowed." He swiveled his bulk toward the wagon where Marsaili stood, gathering the sights around her. Geoffrey placed a restraining hand on his arm.

"We may have trouble," he said, gaining Simon's interest. "The brother-by-marriage is, according to her words, a brute who has hounded her for her favors since before her husband died."

Simon gave a speculative look. "Do you believe

her?"

Geoffrey nodded approvingly. 'Twas why he placed Simon as his captain. Despite the woman's lovely face and figure, and her image as a woman in distress—and one who's life they'd saved—Simon could immediately set the excess aside and focus on the real problem.

Did he believe her?

MARSAILI EYED GEOFFREY and Simon speculatively. She could not hear their voices, but their gaze lingered overmuch in her direction. They either paid scant attention to what they were doing, or wished to keep her in view as they discussed her. To what end? Did they consider a faster pace in the hopes to out-distance Edmund and his ilk? Or did they plan to back-track and turn her over to the evil brute?

She was not sure she trusted Lord de Wylde. Did they believe her?

"Would Milady care for a bit of privacy?"

She met Walter's gaze with a smile. "Aye. A bit of privacy and fresh air would be grand after an hour in that contraption." Sweeping her skirts above the snow, she followed Walter's indication toward a thicket of trees, their bare branches wrapped with leafless vines and other sheltering debris.

After a moment hidden in the copse, testing the knights' scrutiny, she took the opportunity to see to her immediate needs, interested to note Walter kept watch, but did not hurry her.

Long grey shadows planked her path back to the wagon. She paused, giving Hew-the-horse a scratch behind his ears.

"Are ye ready?" Walter asked politely.

"Aye. Can ye give me a leg up?" She tugged her horse's reins free and placed a hand on his neck, positioning herself to be assisted into the saddle.

"She rides with me," Geoffrey rapped out as he approached, a stern look daring her to argue.

"Ye may truly find him dead next time," Marsaili muttered as she flipped her reins into Walter's waiting hand. Squaring her shoulders with a snort of annoyance, she followed Geoffrey into the conveyance, her skin positively twitching, struggling with the effort to bend meekly to his command.

Geoffrey tossed an armful of furs to the bench across from him, reserving the fluffy, comfortable-looking coverlets and thick cushion for his seat.

Propping his leg against a particularly soft pillow, he motioned to the empty bench.

"Please."

Nose in the air, Marsaili swept her skirts aside to avoid touching him and plopped down on the fur-covered board. He flipped a luxurious pelt across her lap then tapped the roof of the wagon once. This time Marsaili was warned and she braced her feet on the floor as the horses hauled the wretched cart into action.

Marsaili waited in silence for the space of ten heartbeats then tossed him a mocking look. "What have ye and Sir Simon decided? Shall we make a dash for the Border, or will we turn back and see what price Edmund will offer for me?"

To her satisfaction, Geoffrey scowled. "I will not barter you for coin," he growled. "And though I have no real confidence you will heed my words of caution, 'twould seem a woman in need of protection—such as yourself—would couch her words in a sweeter tone."

"I've told ye before, Milord. I dinnae need yer protection. I can ride faster without ye slowing me down."

"You have made yourself and your opinion abundantly clear, Milady."

Silence descended upon them and Marsaili sought a way to pass the time. From the rhythm of the horses' hooves and the increasing frequency of jars and shakes, she decided they had indeed picked up the pace. Even if she managed to catch Geoffrey off-guard—and from the eagle-like gaze he kept on her, that seemed hardly likely—she would need a moment to recover from her tumble from the conveyance and a quick step to claim her mount before Simon and Walter gave chase.

She reluctantly discarded her thoughts of escape with a sigh and settled against the back of her seat, wriggling her shoulders deeper into the furs in an attempt to avoid the draughts of cold air that seeped between the boards.

Geoffrey's dark brown eyes stared broodingly at her. She nodded at his propped leg. "How did ye injure it?"

"In battle nearly a year ago," he replied. His hooded gaze offered no further explanation.

Marsaili took a breath and spoke slowly, as to a dullard. "Why does it still pain ye?"

Geoffrey heaved a sigh and conceded to her question. "Because a piece of metal lingers in a spot no physician cares to prod."

She sat upright, interest piqued. "Because ye still enjoy the lasses and do not wish to lose yer function?"

His gaze narrowed. "Because it lies against the bone and next to a very large vessel in my thigh, impertinent wench."

Marsaili winked at him. "I thought as much, though 'twas worth the question to hear yer reply. The injury will one day pain ye so that the operation and its outcome will matter little to ye and ye will have it done."

"You sound certain, Milady. How come you by such knowledge?"

Her mood soured. "I once watched a young man endure a similar procedure. 'Twasnae something I would wish to see again." She dropped her gaze to her lap. "I am no healer."

Geoffrey regarded her for a moment longer. "'Tis the hope of a learned physician that my body will build thick tissue around it and it will cease to be a nuisance to me." He grimaced. "Though the actuality of it has yet to happen, I prefer waiting for healing to a surgical alternative."

Marsaili shrugged. "Surgery is a risky proposition. 'Tis possible he merely placated ye 'til such a time

THE SAINT

as ye would seek another's advice. What man would wish to be the careless physician who maimed or killed The Saint?"

"Many, I would suppose," he returned with a wry look.

She nodded. "Verily. For a man of your consequence, 'twould not surprise me to find those who would be happy to lay claim to such an honor."

Geoffrey raised an eyebrow. "Honor? Though I have killed my share of men, I assure you they have been in battle and would have been most eager to kill me first. I think you overstate the issue."

Marsaili tilted her head back and forth. "Mayhap. But yer reputation is that of a violent man who took to the cloisters in pursuit of his soul."

"I will not be a fighting man again, Milady, as you can see from my enfeebled state. As a younger son, the priesthood was a likely place for me to spend the remainder of my life. Mayhap atoning for some of my earlier deeds, though I tend to think the Lord sees a warrior's duty and aligns Himself with those who closely follow the Chivalric Code."

Marsaili eyed his broad shoulders, his large, muscular body, finding nothing beyond his wound to lend itself to an 'enfeebled state'. Another incongruity struck her. "But ye are *Lord* de Wylde," she puzzled.

"Yes. My two older brothers were killed a month past. One in a joust, the other in a battle on the Border."

Marsaili caught the warning glint in his eye. "I had nothing to do with the border battle, Milord. In fact, I abhor violence and would see the English retire to their side of the Border and cease all hostilities."

"For a woman who carries a small arsenal on her person, I find that rather amusing."

"I dinnae stir up violence, Milord, but I willnae be a willing victim of it, either." She quirked a brow. "Edmund taught me that."

The wagon lurched over the road, tossing Marsaili up and down on the seat. Though the furs Lord de Wylde had accorded her might be warm, they did little to soften the blow of the wooden bench on her behind. An area already sorely abused by her mad dash northward astride her horse two days earlier. She grimaced.

"Would you care to join me?" Geoffrey asked from the smug comfort of his cushions.

Scald his watchful eyes. And blast, but I wish to take

him up on his offer.

"Why do we continue to travel when night is close?" she countered. "Shouldn't we prepare for a stop?"

"I thought you wished to escape Edmund."

She gave a nod. "Ye would push through the night on my behalf?"

"I have considered it."

She leveled him a speculative stare. "I thought ye found it dishonorable I would be driven from my rightful home. To which home are ye taking me? I wish to go home to Scotland, not back to Bellevue. Tell me, Milord. What is the price to see me home?"

CHAPTER SEVEN

C OLD CREPT INTO her bones as the sun disappeared over the horizon. Marsaili ate the hurried supper of bread, cheese and dried meat, washing it down with warmed wine. Lord de Wylde had kept the party moving long past time to seek shelter, and no matter her preference, a make-shift lean-to of thick evergreen branches braced against a rock outcrop and covered with a heavy blanket would be her bower for the night. 'Twas a far cry from the comforts she was accustomed to, but she'd sleep naked on a bed of thorns to avoid Edmund's grasp.

At least we've put more distance between me and Edmund's rabble. She hoped. Marsaili peered over her shoulder at Lord de Wylde and his men as they crouched beside the fire, weapons at the ready.

And it appears they take me seriously.

Though it pains me to repeat myself, Milady, upon my honor, we will not exchange you for money. The memory of Geoffrey's earnest words pierced the mistrust that had shielded her heart for so long. Too much had happened in the past few months to allow her to give her trust freely. Especially to a man.

Damn Edmund!

Her breath caught in her throat as dismay rushed over her. *Why did Edmund have to fix his sights on me? There were lasses aplenty at the castle who cared naught for his brutish behavior and welcomed him into their beds.*

To think one of the *besoms* could rule the home she'd cared for these past five years sent a stabbing pain through her chest. There'd been little comfort in her marriage beside those she created. With a fine stitching hand and an eye for comfortable luxury, she'd formed a beautiful setting for herself and her ladies. Andrew had cared little for her details and left her much to her own devices.

As Lord de Wylde said,'tis my right to retire with dignity to the dower house. But damned if I want to sit by and see my home ruined by one of Edmund's lazy sluts. To her surprise, a wave of homesickness swept over her. She fought the sensation, reminding herself what awaited if she returned to Bellevue.

"If you leave the covering pulled aside, the heat from the fire will keep you warm. One of us will keep the logs burning throughout the night." Geoffrey stood beside her.

Marsaili nodded. "Just as the curtains on my bed hold in the warmth from the hearth at home." She tilted her head. "A bit less privacy than I am used to, but 'twill suffice."

He gave her a wry look, an actual twinkle in his eyes. "I vow 'twill be a bit more than you lying disrobed in my arms before the fire while we breathed life into your gray skin."

Something inside Marsaili shattered at the image of him blowing on her skin. The thought of his lips close to her body sent chills summersaulting through her limbs and she quickly closed her jaw that had gone slack.

"Care to come a bit closer to the fire, Milady?" he asked, his voice courteous as though he hadn't just sent all intelligent notions tumbling out of her brain. He patted his thigh. "I can attest to the benefits of its warmth."

She reined in her wayward thoughts and sought for something, *anything* to say. "Can ye attest to

Wythevede's approval if I leave my seclusion here?" She hated to harp on the old man, but he was the easiest target in her current befuddled condition.

Geoffrey snorted. "After sixty years in my family's service, Wythevede should know his place. It is occasionally unfortunate he believes himself above such notions. But he is very loyal and means well."

"Scant comfort for me," Marsaili noted. She accepted Geoffrey's offer and allowed him to pull her to her feet, trying not to snatch her hand away from the unexpectedly warm, soothing, and utterly powerful sensation of being enveloped in his grasp.

"He will get to know you and direct his loyalty to you, as well." Geoffrey placed a palm at her back in gentle guidance.

"As long as he curbs his *bluttering*," she murmured.

Simon and Walter rose to their feet as Marsaili approached the fire. Wythevede gave a startled glance at the knights' actions and scrambled to his feet, muttering under his breath.

"Keeping yer insults behind yer butter-teeth, Wythevede?" Marsaili breezed as she alighted to the spot indicated on a large log one of the men had dragged before the fire earlier. Lord de Wylde cast a withering look in her direction and seated himself next to her.

Wythevede shoved the knitted cap over his brow and plopped back to his seat, raising his steaming mug to his lips.

"Saint tells us you are returning to your home north of the border, Milady," Walter interjected before Wythevede could muster an answer to Marsaili's question. "I have not been there in many years. What is your home like?"

Marsaili forgot Lord de Wylde's nearness as Walter's question brought back her wariness. "'Tis a small town founded by the Norse almost two centuries ago. 'Twas once called *Loc-hard's by*, but we simply say *Lockardebi* now."

"I was there once," Simon offered with a grin. "Mayhap the tale is not for a lady's ears, but I remember it as a beautiful place, with two rivers."

Marsaili's cheeks heated from more than the crackling blaze, wondering what lass had enticed the angelic-looking knight across the border. "Aye. 'Tis a verra beautiful place. The town's charter was given to Adam de Carlyle by Robert de Brus, Lord of Annandale, almost a hundred years ago."

"And King Henry III considered confiscating the lands several years back, did he not?" Walter asked, leaning toward Marsaili, a curious light in his soft brown eyes.

Simon waved him back. "'Tis no way to talk to a lady, you dolt." He shook his head, turning his attention to Marsaili with excessive courtesy. "How has your family fared, Milady?"

"Well, thank ye," she replied in a prim manner. "Though we could do with less war with the English."

"How long have you lived in England?" Geoffrey asked, turning the conversation smoothly away from Walter's blunder.

"I married Andrew, Lord de Ville, five years ago," she answered. "And if ye wonder if my allegiance is to Scotland or England, my answer is Scotland."

"Sounds as if your years on English soil weren't good ones," Simon interjected.

Marsaili gifted him a brief smile. "My life was as ye could expect, Sir. Though my da meant well, my marriage an English lord did little to create peace on the border. My husband was also a good many years older than I, and though he wished mightily for an heir, none resulted." She spread her hands before her, warming them at the camp fire's flames. "As neither of his two previous wives produced an heir, either, when he passed, the title went to his brother, Edmund."

Geoffrey rested his forearms on his thighs. "Tell me of Edmund."

MARSAILI DROPPED HER gaze to stare into the fire. Geoffrey wondered what she would say. From her earlier actions, it was easy to believe she'd had enough of abuse at Edmund's hands and decided to abandon the life she'd created at Bellevue, returning to Scotland to start anew. But he hadn't been a warrior this long by believing every *fadoodle* he was told. Following Simon's earlier question, he needed to believe her.

And he needed all the information he could gather about the man who may—or may not—be on their trail at this moment.

"Edmund is younger than his brother—my late husband—by several years," she began. "In recent months Andrew's health took a . . . turn for the worse, and Edmund became bolder in his disregard for his brother's wishes, more forceful in his desire to take over the lordship."

Geoffrey studied the woman next to him. Her skin, pale by nature and made lighter by the cold, took on a deadened hue, hiding the normal, healthy glow. Even her cheeks, rosy from the wind, faded.

Marsaili sat in silence and he could only wonder at her thoughts. She curled her fingers into fists and hid them in the folds of her cloak.

"Since he is most insistent I wed him—something I most assuredly dinnae wish to do—I decided to go home." She turned a brilliant smile on the group, indicating her story was at an end. Geoffrey ignored the hint.

"You stated he chased you and would kill you if given the chance. Do you still believe this is true?"

"I doubt Edmund would bother coming after me himself. He isnae likely to risk personal discomfort when he can have another do his bidding whilst he keeps a warm bed and a willing wench in it," she snipped.

That was the Marsaili he knew. Geoffrey almost grinned as he saw color flood her cheeks, then sobered. There was much she did not tell him. How did her late husband's health decline? Disease? Old age? Why did she not petition the king to punish or at least moderate

Edmund's behavior? King Henry wasn't likely to force her to wed her brother-by-marriage, no matter the political impact. Indeed, there was every likelihood he would grant her dower lands and monies from Edmund until she married again. What hold did Edmund have over her that forced her from her home without protection, in the dead of winter?

"Simon, refill her mug," he ordered, handing him the vessel. Simon poured it full of wine, thrusting a red-hot poker into the liquid to warm it. The corners of her lips lifted in thanks, and she wrapped her fingers around the toasty mug.

"Did you consider petitioning the king for your rights as Lord de Ville's widow?" Geoffrey asked casually.

Marsaili gave a slow nod. "Aye."

"Your being a Scot should in no way influence his decision. You were married to an English lord," he added when Marsaili halted with the single word.

"I dinnae believe it would matter where I was born."

"Edmund has that much influence with the king? I have not heard of the man, and I was close to the king for more than a year before my injury."

"Edmund doesnae have to curry favor with the king. He is the new lord at Bellevue, and I am merely a woman."

"Milady, 'tis your right to live your life at Bellevue—"

"So ye've said, Milord," she interrupted, her color now high despite the cold. "As *I've* said, Edmund lives by his own rules."

"How is it he can control you?"

She gave him a piercing stare. "Because he threatened to tell the king I killed my husband."

CHAPTER EIGHT

T HE CAMPFIRE ERUPTED into a thousand sparks of
light. Burning wood scattered outward, away
from the crossbow bolt quivering upright in the center
of the blaze. Simon and Walter sprang to their feet,
weapons drawn.

Geoffrey's hand gripped Marsaili's cloak and the
gown beneath it at the neck. He shoved her backward,
pushing her to the ground behind the log she'd just
been seated on. Her feet flew up in the air and she
clawed frantically for balance, her nails splintering the
rough bark of the old log. The odor of partially rotted
wood and snow clogged her nostrils. She hit the
ground with a soft *umph* and immediately scrambled
into a crouch, peering over the log at the melee.

"Stay." Geoffrey's single word rumbled low.

Men and shadows darted in and out of the firelight.
The scattered brands gave off little light, making it
difficult to tell how many men attacked their group or

who they were. Walter kicked the burning logs back together and the small clearing burst into golden light. He and Simon stood shoulder-to-shoulder, swords swinging, forming a formidable barrier between Marsaili and their attackers. Geoffrey took his stance next to Walter, legs braced apart, giving no evidence of the strain on his injured leg.

Horses whinnied and thrashed in the brush behind them. Wythevede darted past, the light of battle in his eyes as he took charge of the crazed beasts. Marsaili slid her hand into a slit at the side of her skirt and pulled a dagger from the sheath at her thigh. Slipping to her feet, she followed Wythevede into the darkness.

Walter's and Simon's destriers plunged about, secured by their tethers to the picket line. Seeing no one foolish enough to place themselves within striking distance of the enormous hooves, Marsaili glanced further down the line at the other horses. Hew and one of the team strained as far in her direction as their ropes would allow, but the horse on the end danced on his hind feet, his lead clasped in the fist of a man Marsaili did not recognize.

Wythevede clung to the man's back, both skinny legs wrapped around the mail-clad waist. The man spun about in an attempt to dislodge the burden, causing the horse to rear up in panic. Wythevede pounded the man's head with his fists, raining both curses and blows on the unprotected pate. A flat-brimmed metal helmet lay on the ground some feet away and Marsaili grinned.

Good for ye, auld man!

Movement caught her eye. She leaned forward, peering into the shadows, dagger at the ready, clenched in her hand. A second man, dressed much like the first, ducked beneath the picket line, creeping rapidly toward Wythevede. Quickly judging her distance to the man, Marsaili took a step back, placing one foot behind the other and to her left, blading her body toward the man. She flipped the handle-heavy dagger over in her hand and drew her arm back, sending the blade singing past her ear. The dagger slipped from her fingertips at the end of her throw and she stepped forward, adding power to her cast.

The dagger slammed into the man's shoulder at the base of his neck, blood spurting darkly from the wound. He clutched at the blade with a cry as he crumpled to his knees. Wythevede and his soldier startled, glancing backward, pausing almost comically at the sight of the dead man. The warrior recovered first and waved his arms wildly, brushing Wythevede off his back. Stumbling forward, he disappeared into the night, leaving the horse behind.

At the camp, the attacking party faded into the darkness. Bodies lay scattered on the ground, tumbled into awkward positions like piles of children's toys, their strings suddenly severed. Marsaili viewed the carnage with an uncertain eye as she stepped near the fire, her stomach churning at the odor of blood and something more foul.

Geoffrey appeared like the wrath of God at her side and grabbed her roughly, both hands on her upper arms, his eyes wild. "Where were you?" he demanded.

Marsaili tried to brush his hands aside, but he would not be moved. She glared at him, her temper threatening to match his. His grip painful, she gritted her teeth and refused to speak.

"She saved my life!" Wythevede shouted as he sped to her side. "God's teeth, but she can throw a knife!"

Angry enough to spit rivets at Lord de Wylde's handling, Marsaili did not so much as flinch in surprise at Wythevede's unexpected championship. The old man skidded to a stop in the snow beside her, running one hand through his sparse white hair, the other hand braced on his hip.

"I was fighting off one knave when a black-hearted varlet thought to creep up on me." He puffed his chest out as though offended. "Yon *fairhead*," he said, pointing a knobby finger at Marsaili, "threw a *spit-frog* at him, nearly severing his head from his body!" He gave Marsaili an approving look. "Her English husband taught her well."

Marsaili wrenched her arms from Geoffrey's grasp, not certain if she was more offended by his unwarranted actions or Wythevede's assured stance that an Englishman had schooled her in the finer arts of weaponry.

Geoffrey's gaze bore into hers. "You left your position. After I told you to stay." His voice rose and Marsaili thought she saw smoke plume from his nose.

"What do you have to say?" he snarled.

Marsaili lifted her chin, sending Wythevede a withering glance from the corner of her eye. "My *English* husband couldn't teach a pig to eat scraps."

Geoffrey's eyes widened and Marsaili waited for him to collapse to the ground and commence having fits. Instead, he pivoted awkwardly on his good leg and stormed to the center of camp where Walter and Simon sorted through the bodies.

Wythevede nudged her elbow. "Pardon, Milady, but could you teach me how to throw like that?"

GEOFFREY GROUND HIS teeth until he thought he heard a molar crack.

She defies me, then gives me a smart-mouthed answer to a question I didn't ask—and has Wythevede championing her misconduct!

Sharp pain lanced through his leg, rebuking him for his earlier swordsmanship, doubling his anger and frustration. He gripped his thigh and sought a seat on a nearby log, soundly cursing his injury. Simon appeared at his side and crouched close.

"There are five dead. I thought we had one man we could question, but he died only moments after we got to him." He nodded in Marsaili's direction. "Does Milady recognize them?"

Geoffrey worked his mouth but could emit nothing more than a growl. Simon's eyebrows lifted in surprise. He took a longer look at the lady in question, noting Wythevede next to her, engaged in animated conversation.

"Wythevede's manner toward her has changed," he mused, rubbing his chin. "What do you suppose caused that?"

"Bah!" Geoffrey spat, warning glittering in his eyes. "Tell me of the men who attacked us and leave that tittering pair alone."

Simon shot Marsaili and Wythevede a last glance, returning his attention to Geoffrey. "I can tell little from their attire, though they appear to be English, not Scots. No insignia that I've found. All were armored in a random assortment of leather, chain mail, and a few kettle hats among them." He eyed Geoffrey. "Are you sure you don't know what's going on between Wythevede and Milady?"

Geoffrey's breath huffed out. "She saved his life."

Simon canted his head, his interest clear. "And?" he prompted. "What did our lady do? One of the rabble caught sight of her sweet face and stood dumbstruck whilst Wythevede clanged him over the head with a stout limb?"

"She knifed a man who eased up behind Wythevede whilst he fended off a scoundrel who would take the horses." To his surprise, a sense of pride edged its way past the anger in his breast, and he realized he was not furious at her, but at the way he'd felt after the battle when he noticed she was no longer hidden behind the log where he'd left her. One corner of his mouth tugged upward, but he quelled the movement, jamming his eyebrows together fiercely.

"According to Wythevede, she saw the man creep up and threw her dagger at him."

"And she hit him?" Simon's voice rose in wonder.

"Nearly severed his head to hear Wythevede tell the tale. I imagine the knife struck a major artery in the man's neck and he quickly bled to death."

Simon rose to his feet. "I will find out." He called to Walter, and the two strode to the picket line where the horses still snorted and stamped, shying from the smell of blood in the air and the recent violence.

Geoffrey massaged his thigh absently as he watched Marsaili and Wythevede's conversation. Her coolness was a marked contrast to the little man's animated gestures. After a moment, she broke free and strode to Geoffrey.

"A word?" she asked, though she clearly expected him to sit and take whatever she had to say without question.

He motioned for her to be seated. "The accommodations are somewhat sparse, but you are welcome to such as I have."

Marsaili did not accept his offer, but folded her hands before her as though readying to address a particularly recalcitrant servant. He tamped down his rising ire, swearing to listen calmly to what she had to say.

"Milord, I believe the men were sent here by Edmund. I appreciate the fact ye appear to believe I am being followed. For that I thank ye. But I am uncertain our small group can withstand another assault such as this."

He quirked a brow at her. "Is battle-planning another of your skills?" Motioning vaguely at her skirts, he indicated the presence of the daggers he knew were hidden beneath the fabric. "You have admitted to a fine hand with a needle, and demonstrated a bit of skill with a knife. You should speak to Simon about replacing him as my captain."

Her deprecating look nearly drove him insane. "Milord, I understand ye dinnae wish to hear a woman's opinion, but come out from under yer rock and at least admit what I say could be true."

He slapped his thighs with the palms of his hands and rose to his feet, deriving a bit of satisfaction to tower over her. "I have already realized this and will have Wythevede ready the wagon. If he can be persuaded to leave off fawning at your side and attend his duties."

He glanced past her stormy visage, a twinge of remorse at his treatment of her tugging at him. He tempered his voice. "When Walter and Simon have finished admiring your handiwork with a knife, we will take to the road. Dawn isn't far off and lingering is, as you suggest, a poor idea."

He moved past her, but she placed a small hand on his arm. Halting, he gave her a bland look. "Milady?"

"I am sorry ye have such a poor opinion of me," she began, a pained look on her face. "I have run the keep at Bellevue since my marriage, despite Edmund's meddling. I learned not to dither when decisions need to be made, and I do realize a sweet smile oft wins more than a sour visage. However, you and I seem to butt heads at every turn. Please know I appreciate what ye are doing for me."

Geoffrey waited for the rest of her words, bracing for whatever ultimatum she planned. She cocked her head at him, the hint of a smile playing about her lips. The pale light of the waning moon cast its light on the snow, sending a myriad of white sparks twinkling about her. The early morning shadows hid the stains on her gown and her regal bearing lent her the presence of a queen. His fingers itched to smooth the fiery strands of hair from her brow.

"Milord? Have I said something amiss? Would ye accept my apology?"

Geoffrey's lips curled back from his teeth in a feral grin. "That was an apology?" He inclined his head. "My honest mistake. I feared you asked for *my* regrets."

She blinked at him. "They are yer knights, yer wagon and driver. Other than underestimating me, what do ye have to regret?"

Damning the consequences, he snaked an arm around her waist and hauled her against him. Bending his head, he whispered, "This."

CHAPTER NINE

MARSAILI GASPED, THE sound becoming a moan as his mouth covered hers. For a moment she stood paralyzed with shock. Geoffrey's lips caressed, teased, demanded. The tip of his tongue lightly traced the seam of her lips, and they parted without so much as a query to what Marsaili thought was proper.

His tongue nudged hers, inviting it to a mating dance. She accepted, the kiss turning feverish and wild. She leaned closer until there was no space left between them. Her breasts, crushed against his chest, ached with longing, straining against the confines of her gown. Steel-clad arms encircled her, tightening, offering her no chance to escape. With a whimper of sound, she struggled to pull her arms free. His embrace relaxed only a fraction, but it was enough to slide her arms up, wrapping them about his neck, her fingers tangling in his hair.

Her body soared upward on her toes. She pressed

her lips tighter against his, savoring him, consuming him as though she'd forgotten what a man tasted like.

She had.

The ridge nudging against her belly grew harder and Geoffrey's big hands cupped her bottom, fitting her against his length. The heat of him seeped through the layers of fabric between them, and something reckless threatened to unleash inside her.

Geoffrey's hands fell to her waist, holding her in place as he took a step backward. His lips parted from hers and she stared at the storm gathering in his eyes.

"I fear I dinnae understand the English," Marsaili murmured, touching a fingertip to her swollen lips. "Ye dinnae much care for me, yet ye swear to protect me. Ye said ye would regret kissing me, yet I find I dinnae regret it at all."

Geoffrey scowled. "I should not have acted on the impulse. It was inexcusable and wrong. Please accept my most humble apology, milady." He shoved his hands behind his back and Marsaili smiled.

"Dinnae tell me ye arenae astonished to find the snow hasnae melted in a swath about our feet." She pivoted gently and tossed him a look over her shoulder. "'Twas not proper, and it shouldnae happen again."

Damnation! Geoffrey shoved a hand through his hair, gripping his skull as though testing the presence of the brain within.

Why on earth did I kiss the wench? I knew I'd regret it. I even told *her I would.*

But did he?

Her voice taunted him. *It shouldnae happen again.*

But would it?

"Simon! Walter! Make ready to ride." He hobbled closer to the campfire and released some of his frustration by kicking apart the smoldering brands.

"Do we not wait for dawn?" Simon asked as he approached, wiping his blade on a scrap of cloth.

"There is enough moonlight and 'twill be sunrise soon enough." Geoffrey favored him with a scowl. "Or mayhap you wish to wait and see if the scoundrels rally and attack again?"

Simon rammed the cleaned length of sword into its sheath. "With us expecting them this time? They don't stand a chance in hell."

"Let's not stay and find out."

"The team is ready, milord," Wythevede called. "And a warmed stone waiting for you inside the wagon."

Geoffrey's mood took a turn for the worse, finding the overprotectiveness an affront to his status as a knight. His previous status. *Damn his leg.*

Horses whinnied and stamped their hooves, the sounds vivid in the crisp night air. Geoffrey spied his cane lying partly beneath the log he and Marsaili had been sitting on, half-covered by churned snow. Wincing at the pain in his thigh, he snatched up his stick and made his way to the waiting conveyance.

Opening the door, he stepped a booted foot to the threshold and halted. Even in the dim interior, he could see Marsaili seated on the front bench, wrapped in a fur.

"Get her horse," he snapped over his shoulder, not caring who carried out the order.

"But, Saint . . . ." Walter began.

Geoffrey quelled the knight's protest with a look. "She wants exercise."

After Marsaili vacated the cart, the time passed with excruciating slowness. Sunshine cast pale fingers of light through a small window in the door of the wagon which Geoffrey had opened, allowing the biting cold air inside, and torturing him with the sound of

Marsaili's and Wythevede's voices as they chatted back and forth. Occasionally, Simon and Walter joined them, and Geoffrey huddled deeper into his furs and self-castigation.

I had no right to kiss a woman under my protection. She should never feel it is a condition of her safety. I have broken my sworn oath as a knight and my studied vows at the monastery.

The conveyance pitched and tossed over the rocky road, jarring his leg, the pain setting his teeth on edge. Wythevede finally pulled the team to a stop and opened the wagon's door, his cold-reddened face wreathed in a smile, tufts of white hair sticking out from his cap.

"Milady wished a break and a bite to eat, Milord," he said, moving back to allow Geoffrey room to step down. "And the weather looks to be taking another turn for the worse." The old man struck the doorframe with his fist. "Damn, but milady can sit a horse!"

Geoffrey glanced up as Marsaili walked past, her horse following. "Dinnae think my English husband taught me to ride," she warned, a merry lilt to her voice.

Geoffrey stared at her as though she were the first

drop of water he'd seen after a week in the desert. She tied her horse to the back of the wagon and brushed her gloved hands together, giving him a bright smile.

"I'm starved."

I am, too. He gripped the top of his cane, ignoring the throbbing pain in his leg as the ache in his groin took precedence. *But not for food.*

"May I have a word, Milady?"

"Of course. Though I should help Sir Simon prepare a small meal." She peered at the sky. "Walter has gone ahead to seek shelter. I dinnae like the look of the sky."

"Marsaili."

She stared at him in surprise. "Milord?"

They were alone. Wythevede had pulled the team across the small clearing and busied himself watering the horses. Simon dug through his pack, four mugs placed on the ground next to him.

"I should apologize for making you ride this morning instead of joining me in the wagon."

Marsaili tossed her head, her red-gold hair straying from its braid, glinting in the sun. The cold and exercise tinted her creamy skin with roses, and her eyes sparkled. "Ye *should* apologize, but 'tis clear ye willnae.

But ye likely cast me out for my own good, aye?"

He could have lied, but he didn't. "No. For my own good. After I kissed you, I did not want to ensconce myself in the wagon with you. I had taken unfair advantage of you and I did not want it to happen again."

Marsaili propped a hand on one hip. "Are ye saying ye cannae control yerself around me? 'Tis a weighty thing to think on, ye being a saint and all."

His eyes narrowed. "Are you finished punishing me, or shall I bare my back for more of your tongue's lashes?"

The thought of running her tongue over his muscled back took the wind out of her sails. She flipped her fingers at him and strolled toward Simon, her voice trailing behind her. "Och, dinnae fash, Milord. 'Tis forgotten and forgiven."

FORGIVEN? OCH, 'TIS naught to forgive, but Milord seems anxious to receive absolution and I see no harm in granting it.

Forgotten? Not in a thousand years!

She gave Simon a small smile and began pouring

wine into the mugs, her thoughts far from the task. *Had Andrew kissed me like that I'd have enjoyed marriage far more.* The memory of Geoffrey's chiseled lips on hers sent a ball of warmth pooling low in her belly. She closed her eyes, savoring the rich taste of the man—a bit of cinnamon from the last of the bread they'd brought from the inn, the savory spice of the dried meat they'd eaten for supper, and the lush taste of wine . . . .

Wine! Her eyes flew open, aghast at the sight of the deep red liquid cascading over the rim of the mug. She tilted the flagon up, halting the flow, and glanced up, meeting Simon's curious stare.

"Is aught amiss, Milady?" he asked. "I hope the memory was worth the loss of good wine."

The heat in her belly vanished and Marsaili touched fingertips to her cheeks, hoping they weren't as flaming red as she feared.

"Try this mug," Simon prodded, placing an empty one before her. He took a swig from the over-filled cup and set it aside. Marsaili carefully poured the rest of the wine.

"He isn't really a saint, Milady."

Marsaili startled, the flagon nearly slipping from

her fingers. "What . . . why do ye say that?"

Simon shrugged. "He has never been quite like other men, 'tis true. He's always had a very definite view of what was right and wrong." He brushed the snow from a large rock and motioned for her to sit, and Marsaili smoothed her skirts beneath her, perching on the cold stone. Simon leaned comfortably against a tree, arms crossed over his chest.

"His brothers were terrors, but not The Saint. As boys, the older boys' pranks were legendary. And as they became young men, there was not a woman within miles who was safe from their attentions— though they wouldn't have forced themselves on any of them. No, they simply attracted every female they came in contact with and turned none away."

"And his lordship is a monk?" Marsaili asked drolly. It wasn't possible he kissed like that without practice. A lot of practice.

"Nay, simply very selective. He doesn't allow himself to behave outside the code of chivalry. He will not take advantage of anyone, and if a merchant's scales give him an overage, he will note and pay the difference."

"If his brothers were such rapscallions, where did

he come by his beliefs?"

"I don't know if there was a particular act that created the man. My thought is he saw the true results of the pranks and the broken hearts his brothers left behind and it pained him. He doesn't see women as persons to be used and cast aside. He truly cares for people."

"And that's why he's helping me?" Marsaili abandoned the memory of Geoffrey's arms wrapped around her and headed for a somewhat safer topic.

"Yes. You are a woman who has been forced to flee a man's unwanted attentions, abandoning your home and your livelihood to escape. He is rescuing you, though you have rather completely destroyed the peaceful life he'd thought to create for himself."

"As a border lord, he'd have to be daft to think his life will be peaceful," she scoffed.

"You have a point, Milady, but after so much battle, he'd retired to the monastery to heal and give the rest of his life to God."

"You and Sir Walter remained with him there?"

"No. We stayed in service at Belwyck and were sent to retrieve him when his brothers were killed and The Saint became Lord de Wylde."

"So ye dinnae know what treatment he has had for his leg?"

"I know the tip of a very ill-made arrow pierced his leg, breaking off when it struck bone. Saint, Walter and I and several others were on a hunt. A boar attacked two of the horses ahead of us. One of the riders shot at the beast with his crossbow, but the shot went wild. I removed the arrow from The Saint's leg and staunched the wound while he watched from atop his horse. As soon as I finished, he continued with the hunt, though he suffered a fever later that led to his decision to retire."

Simon canted his head to the side. "I do not know what was done for him once he arrived at the monastery. Walter and I were summarily dismissed, and since it seemed he was to be there for at least the foreseeable future, we returned to Belwyck. Why do you ask?"

Marsaili worried her lower lip. "My husband also suffered a wound and slowly died from it. I dinnae believe his was an accident."

CHAPTER TEN

S IMON'S FACE GRAYED. "Do you see similarities between The Saint's wound and your husband's?"

Marsaili thought hard. "It appears Lord de Wylde is recovering, though until the metal is removed, 'tis doubtful he will be free of the pain or have full use of his leg. Andrew's recovery was met with several obstacles, and after an additional incident, he began his decline."

"What caused the initial injury?" Simon asked.

She played with the folds of her skirt, gathering her thoughts. "Andrew was a scholarly man. He disliked war—and in that respect, he and I got along well. But Edmund always pushed him, telling him the villagers dinnae want their lord to read books, and wanted a fighting man instead. As far as I could tell, the people preferred a peaceful lord to a warring one, but Edmund dinnae agree, and I quickly learned 'twas not worth a bruise to oppose him."

Marsaili rose and began to pace. "Edmund often provoked Andrew to spar with him. They had each trained with the sword as lads, but Andrew withdrew to his library after their da died and he received the title. On this particular day, Edmund had apparently angered Andrew more than usual, and their sparring took on heated tones. By the time I was summoned to the hall, a crowd had gathered and the two men had been fighting for some time. I was told Andrew had ripped a sword from a selection of ancient arms hung on the wall—he never carried a sword himself—and appeared bent on making Edmund apologize for whatever he'd said."

She faced Simon and halted, her arms crossed beneath her breasts. "To my surprise, he pounded Edmund fiercely, and Edmund lost his sword. He quickly claimed another from those on the wall, and, during a riposte, lost his footing. With what appeared to be sheer luck, his sword plunged into Andrew's side."

Simon's brow furrowed. "That can be a difficult wound to recover from. In truth, Edmund could be held responsible for his brother's death."

Marsaili nodded. "Aye. For I believe 'twas no accident his sword pierced his brother's flesh. But 'twas I who nursed him."

Snow crunched beneath booted feet and limbs rustled, depositing their loads of snow in a flurry of white. Marsaili and Simon looked up as Lord de Wylde stepped near. At the other edge of the clearing, Wythevede gripped the horses' reins.

Three men burst through the thicket, their arms bound behind them. Walter, atop his destrier, prodded their steps. They halted before Geoffrey. Simon drew his sword and stood at Geoffrey's shoulder. Tension sang in the cold air.

The Saint eyed the men, their roughened appearance announcing Walter had taken exception to any dispute they'd offered. A thin line of blood snaked down the side of one man's face, either dried or frozen in the frigid air. Two had ripped clothing, and one had lost his boot. The boldest of the three returned Lord de Wylde's stare, a sly smile on his face as he caught sight of Marsaili.

"Here, Milord. No reason for us to be at odds. I'm sure the wench is troublesome and of no use to you. You can hand her over and we'll be on our way."

Geoffrey's inscrutable gaze lingered on the coarse

man. "I fear you ask the impossible. *Milady* is with us and will remain so until she is safely home."

The man spat on the ground, his grin gone. "We've been sent to retrieve her and she's led us on a merry chase in this god-forsaken weather."

Geoffrey leaned forward, his cloak billowing in the rising wind. "Consider this your only warning. Without paperwork proving your claim to her, you are considered hostile to a woman I have sworn to protect. If you persist, you will be dealt with harshly."

"My claim is good." The man jerked his head at Walter. "Check the bag he took from me. It says I am to return to Bellevue Castle with one runaway Lady de Ville, giving her over to Lord de Ville." He nodded. "That's her."

Walter tossed the rough hide bag to Simon who jerked it open and rummaged inside. He withdrew a roll of velum and handed it to Geoffrey.

Spreading the single page open, Geoffrey scanned the scratchy writing. He took a moment to study the rather hastily stamped wax seal at the bottom beneath a scrawled signature.

Edmund, Lord de Ville.

"He is welcome to make his argument known in

person at Castle Belwyck when I am in attendance. Tell him to bring a writ from the king."

He shoved the vellum at Simon who returned it to the bag. Nodding at Walter, he commanded, "Cut them free but do not return their weapons."

The spokesman for the trio sputtered. "Milord! What if we meet with ruffians on the road?"

Geoffrey spared him a sharp glance. "Such as yourself? I'd suggest you make haste."

Walter dismounted and sliced their bonds with a small dagger he pulled from a sheath on his gauntlet. The men rubbed their arms, scowling at the weapons protruding from the pack on the knight's destrier, completely out of their reach.

Walter unsheathed his sword and motioned them away. "Lord de Wylde said to make haste. You should listen. Milord is always right."

The men's actions stilled. "Lord de Wylde? We know the name. Which son is he?"

Simon took a step forward. "He is The Saint."

SOMETIME LATER, MARSAILI burrowed her hands in the plush fur spread across her lap. Uncomfortable in the pitching and rolling conveyance and bored to the point of distress, she tried conversation as a means of distraction from her woes.

"Ye arenae speaking much. Do ye not think a word or two would be better than brooding over something ye dinnae understand?"

The wagon stuttered over a series of ruts and Geoffrey gripped the walls, his knuckles white. "What do you think I don't understand?" he asked.

"Depending on where ye wish to take this conversation, I'd say one thing ye dinnae understand is why Edmund is so persistent. There are plenty of women eager for the title and duties of Lady de Bellevue. Why not choose one of them?"

"Why doesn't he?"

Marsaili sighed heavily. "I dinnae know. I have asked myself that question many times in the past months. My best guess is he is a bully who doesnae want what is easily his, but craves that which he cannae have."

"And months of chasing you has not cooled his ardor?"

"Why do some men act thus?" she returned. "Instead of crying off and pursuing someone who shows interest, why must they persist where they arenae wanted?"

The wagon jarred again, almost sending Marsaili to the floor. Geoffrey bounced on his seat, unable to bite back a cry. Instantly, Marsaili leapt to her feet, banging on the roof of the wagon to gain Wythevede's attention. She knelt on the floor next to Geoffrey, placing her hand on his arm.

"Milord, ye dinnae look so good. Is it yer leg?"

"Stop this damn box," he ground out between gasps. Sweat popped on his brow and a white line of pain edged his lips.

Wythevede hauled the team to a stop. A moment later, he appeared at the door. Marsaili shook her head at his open-mouthed look of surprise, knowing how her position on the floor, her head nearly in his lap, must look to the man.

"Help me get him comfortable on this bench. We wait the storm out here."

Simon shoved Wythevede aside and stuck his head in the doorway. "Is aught amiss, Milady?" His gaze went to Lord de Wylde. "What has happened?"

"One too many bumps in this torture chamber," Marsaili replied briskly. "He must rest. How far are we from the shelter Walter found?"

"Not far, but we can wait a bit. The storm seems to be passing by. But it will be good to have walls around us overnight. We will be at Belwyck by mid-day tomorrow."

Geoffrey gripped Marsaili's hand. "I can make it to the shelter. No need to wait."

Marsaili turned her attention to Geoffrey. "We will take a short break, Milord, whilst ye make yerself comfortable. I willnae let Wythevede take it at more than a snail's pace, but even that isnae without bumps." She motioned to Simon. "Pack the cushions beneath him, especially his leg, and wrap the furs about him. I will sit with him when I return."

"Where are you going, Milady?" Simon asked.

She quirked an eyebrow at him. "'Tis impolite to ask, but he isnae the only one who needs a wee break."

She exited the wagon and Simon stepped inside. Wythevede jumped in front of her, his cap in his hands.

"What will happen to Milord?" he asked, eyes round with worry.

Marsaili patted his hands. "Dinnae fash. Milord's leg pains him and he needs a moment to collect himself." She tilted her head at the wagon. "Simon needs yer help. Be strong. Milord doesnae like to pamper his leg and is likely to be a bit testy."

Leaving Wythevede, she called to Walter. "Simon and Wythevede are making Lord de Wylde more comfortable. We will continue in a moment."

When she returned to the wagon, Simon helped her climb aboard. He met her questioning look with a vague shrug of his massive shoulders, and she stepped inside, fearing the worst.

Lord de Wylde glared at her from his cocoon of furs, but it was an improvement over the unfocused look he'd given her earlier when his sole concern had been the pain in his leg. Marsaili smiled reassuringly at him and sat on a pile of blankets on the floor.

"Ye overdid it last night when ye fought the rabble," she said softly.

"You would prefer I let them have you?" he asked, his tone mild.

Marsaili's heart warmed. She'd have thought he'd be furious with her for taking charge and telling him and his men what to do. But he seemed to know she only wished to help. Whether he appreciated it or not was another topic, but she would save that for a later day.

With a creak of the wooden wheels, the wagon

moved slowly forward, taking each rut, dip and stone with unhurried ease. "At this rate we'll reach Belwyck a week or two before I die of old age," Geoffrey quipped with a slight twitch of his lips.

Marsaili searched his face anxiously, but though his brow furrowed and his jaw remained firm, the tell-tale white rim of pain around his lips was gone. "We will warm ye up and let yer leg rest, then be on our way on the morrow."

"I'm sweltering now," he complained.

She brushed his brow with the back of her hand. "Ye dinnae appear feverish. 'Tis likely ye are bundled a wee bit too tight." She pulled the edges of the pelts apart, allowing cool air to caress his neck and shoulders. The sway of the wagon rocked Geoffrey side-to-side and Marsaili braced herself against his hip to steady him. Her gaze glided over his bundled form, lingering on his chest. It was covered with his woolen shirt and framed in plush fur, but she remembered the rock-hard feel of his muscles against her breasts.

Her hand splayed against his shirt, the heat of him drawing her closer. She lightly pressed down, her palm encountering a springiness beneath the fabric that bespoke a hairy chest. Andrew's had been smooth.

What would it feel like to run her fingers through the wiry hairs on Geoffrey's chest?

Lost in her musing, she slid her hand up, cupping his square chin and day's growth of beard in her palm. His lips curved upward and her gaze flew to his eyes. They glowed, searching her soul.

"Still no fever?" he queried.

Marsaili swallowed past the lump in her throat. "Nae. Yer skin is warm, but not overly so."

"Brooding?"

"What do ye mean?" Her hand lingered on his cheek.

"You aren't saying much. Better to talk than brood, I believe you mentioned."

She blinked, struggling to make sense of what he said. Of course. Their earlier conversation. She'd been seeking a way to keep her mind from wandering down sensual paths it had no right to take. But she no longer wished to discuss Edmund or what his reasoning may or may not be. She gazed into his liquid amber eyes.

"What else do you think I do not understand, milady?" he prompted, his breath warm against her hand.

Her gaze fell to his lips.

"This."

CHAPTER ELEVEN

MARSAILI ROSE ON her knees, leaning close as she slowly lowered her face to his. For a brief moment their breaths mingled, and she ached to press her lips against his. His hand slid from beneath the layers of fur and captured her wrist. With a sharp tug, he pulled her against him, and Marsaili offered no resistance.

Her lips molded to his, perfectly, as though they'd been made only for him. They moved against his, pledging a hundred things she could not voice. Regaining her balance, she cradled his face in her palms as though she feared he would leave her before she'd drank her fill. His lips parted, his tongue twining sensuously with hers, and Marsaili's world came apart.

His hand slid up her arm, pushing its way inside her cloak, stopping to cup the fullness of her breast. She gasped as his thumb rubbed the sensitive peak, creating friction that exploded through her into shards of need. His other hand broke free of the furs and he palmed the back of her head, his fingers winnowing through her hair.

She moaned against his mouth and Geoffrey abandoned her breast, reaching behind her, fingers fumbling with the lacings at her back. Jerking them free, he loosened the gown over her shoulders, drawing it forward until the neckline gaped downward. Breaking their kiss with a groan, he cupped both hands beneath her breasts, spilling them over the top of her dress. Marsaili's exposed flesh tingled in the cold air, and in the heat of his hungry gaze.

She shifted slightly, bringing her breasts closer, offering them to him. He accepted, running his mouth over the sensitive skin, circling the rigid crests with his tongue. His heated breath played havoc with Marsaili's insides, twisting them like a banner in a tempest.

Raking the sleeves of her dress down from her shoulders, he scooped her breasts free, hefting them gently in his warm palms. "My God, Marsaili! You are perfect."

His admiration wrung a wry smile from her as it sparked less-than-fond memories. "'Tis kind of ye to say so, Milord," she whispered.

"There is no kindness meant, but the very truth. You cannot begin to imagine how much you fascinate me." He smoothed his fingers over the tops of her breasts. "Though I confess I still do not understand."

Marsaili sagged backward, finding a comfortable niche in the crook of his elbow. "What do ye not understand, Milord?"

Geoffrey's eyes darkened and he tilted her chin upward until their lips met. "This."

THE SWAY OF the wagon settled as it eased to a halt. Voices rose, growing louder. With a muffled shriek, Marsaili slipped from her half-sprawl across Geoffrey's chest and landed on the floor of the wagon, her back to the door. Geoffrey yanked the hem of his tunic down, regretting the loss of her hands on his skin, and pulled the edges of the furs across his over-heated body.

"Easy, Marsaili," he murmured, hiking the fold of a dense pelt over the aching ridge of his bulging manhood.

She shot him a look from the corner of her eye distinctly at odds with the passionate woman he'd held in his arms only moments before. Jerking her gown into place, she reached behind her for the laces. She fumbled beneath the heavy fabric of her cloak, her face growing redder as she struggled.

With a sigh, Geoffrey tossed his coverings aside and sat, leaning over her. "Let me," he offered. Before he could decide if she was going to punch him or allow him to help, the wagon's door opened, and Wythevede stuck his head inside.

Geoffrey turned smoothly, reaching for his cane as he rose to his feet, blocking the old man's gaze. Crouching, he angled out the door, then turned back and reached inside for Marsaili.

She batted his hand away. He leaned in and caught her arm, pulling her gently but firmly to his side. She met his gaze with a flash of her eyes, and he noted her almost uncomfortably upright posture. Casually sliding a hand beneath her cloak, he splayed a hand at her back, encountering rumpled cloth and jumbled laces.

"The old hut only has three walls, Milord," Wythevede whined. "I can only hope the roof doesn't cave in on us during the night."

"'Twill be sufficient," Geoffrey replied. "Walter has done an excellent job with what he has been accorded." He jerked his head at the horses. "See to it they are watered and fed, then bring them to the opening in the wall. They can enjoy the protection of the roof and form somewhat of a barrier at the same time."

Wythevede beamed at him. "Excellent suggestion, Milord! I will take care of it now."

Gripping the edges of Marsaili's gown closed beneath the cover of her cloak, Geoffrey gave her a small bow. "Let us repair your disarray and see what Walter and Simon have for us to dine on this night. 'Twill be warmer inside, and our absence noted if we remained without."

Together, they stepped inside the partially destroyed hut. Simon glanced up from preparing their evening meal and Walter stomped past with an armful of wood for the fire. Geoffrey gave Simon a curt nod.

"A mug of heated wine as soon as you can, please," he said as he moved behind Marsaili, taking advantage of the shadows to mask his actions. Within seconds he had the back of her dress laced and tied, her cloak smoothly in place. She thanked him with a grim smile and walked to the fire, hands over the flames. Simon handed her a mug and she accepted the offering, wrapping her fingers around it as she sipped.

Walter tossed a stack of pelts over a pile of fresh-cut pine boughs. "This is your space, Milady," he said. "I hope you are comfortable this night. We cannot give you much privacy, as I've placed you between us and the fire for your protection." He gave her a helpless shrug. "We'll try to keep our backs to you."

Marsaili laughed softly and touched his arm. "My thanks, sir knight. I have no fear for my person with ye and Sir Simon close by." She slanted a look over her shoulder at Geoffrey. "Mayhap ye could form a comfortable spot for Lord de Wylde, also. He's having a difficult time keeping his mind off the pain in his leg."

"A night on the cold, hard ground would not be as pleasant as one spent in a soft-bosomed embrace," Geoffrey noted, pleased to see Marsaili's cheeks redden at his innuendo.

Walter obligingly scattered springy boughs on the ground several feet away and dropped furs atop the pile, looking to Geoffrey for approval.

Geoffrey waited for Marsaili's reply, but none came. "Though the cold ground is perchance my penance for some disreputable action in my not-so-distant-past."

Walter fisted his gloved hands on his hips. "Do you

want the boughs or not, Milord?"

Geoffrey held Marsaili's gaze a moment longer then turned to the knight. "Yes, thank you. I'll take the first watch after we sup."

MARSAILI SAT ON her pallet, pleased with the springiness of the boughs Walter had cut. She sipped a mug of hot wine, letting its warmth course through her insides. The fire Simon tended gave off a pleasant heat and the horses' heavy bodies added a musky warmth to the room.

She ran the tip of her tongue over her lips, remembering the taste of Geoffrey's skin.

This has gotten out of hand. He cannae possibly want me. And even if he did, I must get to Scotland and out of Edmund's reach.

Marsaili couldn't say what exactly it was that drew her to Lord de Wylde. Her only experience with men had been casual indifference from Andrew and repulsive lust from Edmund. The others at Bellevue and the nearby village had kept their distance. In part from the lack of desire to incur Andrew's wrath at giving too much attention to what was his, and part because of her Scot's heritage. Though Bellevue nestled at the farthest reach of the Borders, nearly every family had lost someone to the wars, and Marsaili understood she was only a sacrifice to the elusive delusion of peace. No one, least of all she, was required to like having a Scot in their midst.

She allowed her mind to linger over Lord de Wylde's features. They certainly were enough to interest a woman. Even though he wore minimal armor, his broad shoulders and thickly muscled arms and legs bespoke the rigorous lifestyle of a warrior. The past months of recovery at the monastery appeared to have done nothing to soften his appearance. His hawk-like dark amber eyes were often inscrutable—when he wasn't undressing her with his gaze. 'Twas a peculiar sensation. Edmund had done it often enough, but Lord de Wylde made her feel singularly significant. As though the man beheld a banquet and wished to indulge his senses and hers. Beneath Edmund's lustful drool, she'd felt like a common meal—quickly eaten and perhaps tossed into a convenient ditch later if it didn't suit.

But what perplexed her the most, beyond her own overwhelming interest in the man, was his attitude.

Cool to her in the beginning, he'd nonetheless cared for her and took her under his protection. Though she'd certainly not wanted his help, he'd held fast to his code and she quite possibly owed her life to him. There was no guarantee Edmund's men wouldn't have caught up with her before she reached Lokardebi, despite her greater speed on her own. The thought was enough to cause her blood to run cold.

Though there'd been sparks between them, it had taken Lord de Wylde's first kiss to see her utterly undone. And she certainly couldn't blame their nearness in the wagon for her boldness later. She'd had none of the nurturing feelings of a healer toward a patient. No, there was something about the man that caused her to lose all reason. It both intrigued her and frightened her to death.

I'll simply make sure the occasion doesnae occur again. 'Tis certain we can manage to conclude our journey in politeness and without rancor. Satisfied with her decision, Marsaili set her mug aside and curled on her make-shift bed, inhaling the tang of pine beneath the thick furs.

Even if he wishes to explore this madness further, I will simply explain to him why our relationship can go no further. I am going home to Scotland, and he is an English border lord. Other than a few passionate kisses, we have nothing in common.

Nothing at all.

CHAPTER TWELVE

G RAY CLOUDS MASKED the sun, permitting passage of pale light but little warmth. Wind blasted in frigid gusts around Marsaili, dipping its icy fingers inside her cloak. Even with one of the furs from the wagon wrapped about her and snuggly tied, she couldn't escape the dreary day and for the hundredth time wished she'd not insisted on riding Hew. Wythevede had trundled three nice-sized stones into the wagon, smoke rising from them before he'd wrapped each in a pelt. Inside the conveyance was the warmth she craved. But therein was also Lord de Wylde.

She huddled deeper within the fur. *At least his lordship probably has warm feet. I dinnae think I can feel mine.*

Simon had warmed some wine before they left the hut and added it to an empty flagon, giving it to her to place beneath her cloak. The heat had been very welcome, but the wine was quickly cooling in the wintery weather and Marsaili's mood was suffering as well.

Though the men had each taken a turn at watch during the night, they attended their morning duties pleasantly, seemingly undeterred by the blustery weather or their lack of sleep. Marsaili envied them their indifference, though they appeared warm enough beneath their armor, and she had no one but herself to blame for declining a seat in the wagon. Herself and Lord de Wylde.

"Are you well, Milady?" Simon asked, reining his horse close to hers. Marsaili startled out of her dark thoughts, but her horse plodded on undeterred, head down against the snow hurled back into the air by the wind.

She nodded, both hands tucked beneath her cloak for warmth. There was little fear Hew would bolt more than a few steps in the drifts. They'd all realized from the outset the icy ground was no place for a gait faster than a steady walk.

"We should arrive at Belwyck in another hour or so," he added. "There will be a fire in the hearth and a hot drink waiting."

Marsaili knew he meant to encourage, but she was miserable and couldn't summon the effort to find pleasure in his words. Fire and comfort seemed a very long time away. She frowned. "How can ye tell? We've scarcely seen the sun today. It could be the morrow and we'd not know it."

Simon laughed. "Milady, we have been traveling for the better part of the morning and the sun will be directly overhead soon. Would you care to ride in the wagon, now? 'Tis a bumpy ride, but at least sheltered."

"'Tis not the bumps that worry me," she replied darkly.

"Has The Saint given you cause to worry?" Simon asked. "He is not known for a sense of humor and could be a disagreeable traveling companion in his present state. His injury bothers him sorely. 'Tis quite a change for a man used to riding at the head of the column and completely in command."

"Och, I wouldnae call him *disagreeable*." Marsaili tried for a charitable tone, but Simon regarded her curiously, a brow arched as though a thought had dawned on him.

"Are you attracted to the man? He has been kind to you, and you have been through much tumult of late."

Marsaili fought the urge to fling her dagger at the knight. He likely meant well, but to think she would develop feelings for Lord de Wylde simply because he'd been kind to her . . . . Gritting her teeth, she forced a smile.

"I dinnae fall at the feet of every man who has a kind word for me, Sir Simon, no matter how few there have been. Lord de Wylde doesnae treat me with kindness. He treats me within his code. I am a point of honor to him. Neither more nor less."

She cringed to deliver the bold lie, but there could be no mistake she and Lord de Wylde were not attracted to each other. Since Simon seemed well-acquainted with the details of his lordship's life, quelling his guess was in her best interest.

Simon gave a slow nod. "He is fair to everyone. And a difficult man to get to know. You have only been with him a couple of days and he has been troubled by the travel and the weather. He will be a different man once we arrive at Belwyck."

"I sincerely hope so," she muttered.

"I beg pardon, Milady?" Simon leaned closer as though to hear her better.

Marsaili lifted her chin. "I shan't linger long. No

need to concern yerself with Lord de Wylde's actions on my behalf. I am sure he will have much to do when he arrives. He'll likely have forgotten all about me within an hour or so."

LORD DE WYLDE kicked the furs aside with his good leg. *Prideful wench. She is by now likely regretting not accepting my offer of a seat in the wagon.* He scrubbed the back of his neck with one hand. He could have commanded her presence, but her cool response had taken him aback, and he'd left her mounting her horse, snow dancing about her.

She is right. We do not need to spend time alone again. Though she captivates me, our time is soon at an end and I will not compromise her honor further. My own is in jeopardy for not being able to offer her solitude in the wagon. Damned leg. He sighed and placed his head in his hands, away from the wall that jostled with every misstep the heavy wheels took, giving over to the memory of the woman who even now tempted him to abandon the right path he knew lay before him.

Her fiery hair bespoke her temper when riled, but that same temperament created a passion he'd not found in any other woman. Though he'd pledged a solitary, quiet life now that his injury precluded military pursuits, he found her spirit rather suited him. He smiled at the impertinence, her most distinguishing trait.

'Twas not proper and it shouldnae happen again.

His grin widened. Their first kiss hadn't been proper and shouldn't have happened again. But it had, and he couldn't bring himself to feel remorse. Though he'd likely do a lengthy penance once things were settled at Belwyck and he made his confession, he honestly didn't care and would welcome the chance to kiss Marsaili again—should she wish it. Though this time their embrace would be in guaranteed privacy and with clear expectations spelled out for each of them. Passionate kissing and fondling was well and good, but hardly where he wanted things to end.

He pushed the wooden panel on the door aside and glanced at the sky. Leaden clouds hung low. The narrow view between the slats showed him little more than blustery gusts of drifting snow that nearly obscured the trees along the edge of the road. Icy air pushed its way inside the conveyance and Geoffrey shut the window to keep the cold at bay. Settling into the furs and bracing his leg against one of the warm, fur-wrapped stones, he schooled his thoughts to what lay ahead for him at Belwyck, and away from the luscious body of the woman who threatened the peace he desired.

BELWYCK CASTLE LOOMED ahead. Two stone towers flanked the metal-studded gate. Part of the wall was of enormous, hewn timbers, but Marsaili noted it was being replaced by a perimeter of stones thicker than the length of her horse. Black shadowed lines under-scored the top-dressing of snow atop the gray boulders.

The gates opened, a ponderous movement due to their size. A ramp lowered across the moat surrounding the castle, its still waters as black as ink. Chains creaked and clattered a discordant welcome to the group and a banner appeared over one tower, an-nouncing Lord de Wylde was again in residence. Walter had unfurled a similar banner a short time earlier and it billowed and snapped in the wind.

Marsaili shifted nervously in her saddle as she rode through the barbican, the sun utterly absent in the tunnel, the only light created by smoking torches clamped to the walls.

'Tis more like a dungeon than an entry into a castle. But the thick stone blocked the wind and the torches blazed with heat. Just as her fingers and toes began to thaw, the party exited the barbican into the bailey where churned mud and more snow greeted them.

Anonymous figures of men and women, bundled tight against the weather, scattered about the open area, hugging the walls, as far from the wind as possible. Boys darted across the muddy yard from a low building, taking charge of the horses. One of the lads tossed Marsaili a cheeky grin as he took Hew's reins, his cheeks blistered by the elements, eyes alight with mischief beneath a knitted cap.

Marsaili slowly unbent her stiff arms and legs, her gloved hands fumbling with the reins and mane, cloak and furs. Gauntleted hands grasped her waist, hauling her from Hew's back. She stumbled as her numb feet registered the ground beneath them and Simon's grip held her steady. Too cold to care what the residents of Belwyck Castle thought of her, she nonetheless scanned the hooded faces. But scant attention was paid to her as all eyes were riveted to the wagon as Lord de Wylde emerged.

He straightened and, placing his cane on the ground even with his right leg, stepped forward. The castle's denizens stared at him dispassionately as he halted before them.

"Thank you for your welcome. Please take yourselves inside and keep out of the weather. I will settle in and I am sure there will be ample chance for us to meet under better circumstances. Direct your inquiries to Sir Simon in my stead for the immediate future."

He gave a short nod of dismissal and the crowd dispersed, shuffling from the bailey into their respective buildings. He stared after them for a few moments, then turned to Simon.

"We should all be indoors with something to warm our insides." He motioned toward a large door in the side of the keep. "Milady."

Marsaili drank in the sight of him, tall and muscular, leaning heavily on his cane. His dark hair glistened in the pale sunlight and his amber eyes pierced hers as though asking if she'd had a change of heart. Lifting her chin, Marsaili gathered her skirts and turned her back on him, denying the plea in her heart to indulge even once more in his embrace. She would be gone on the morrow and in her heart she knew there would be no more kisses and touches between them. Next time—and there would not be a next time—their passion would take them on a far different route. One she could not afford to travel.

She picked her way carefully over the clumps of ice and ruts made in the frozen slush. Twice her boots slipped on the precarious surface, but she righted herself with Sir Simon's help. The door to the keep opened and a squat man stepped out, quickly closing the door behind him. His head was covered in a massive fur cap and a lined cloak draped about his sturdy form.

"My name is Gavan de Langton. I am the steward here. Come inside, Milady. A place will be found for you." He straightened, staring over her shoulder at the men behind her. "Your room is ready, Milord, and accommodations made for your men. A great feast is being prepared to celebrate your arrival, and refreshments await you inside."

Marsaili reached the wide stone steps before the door and paused to glance once more at Lord de Wylde. She would, of course, decline the feast. There was no reason to draw further attention to herself, and she would need her rest for the journey tomorrow.

Other than making her request for Lord de Wylde to fulfill his promise to send her on her way across the border with an escort—which she hoped to do by messenger and spare her tempting time in his presence—this could be the last time she laid eyes on him.

Lord de Wylde strode forward. His cane slid deep into an icy rut, sinking in the slush created by the passage of man and beast. Caught fast in the ruthless mud, the slender wooden cane tore free from his grip and he stumbled forward, his injured leg unable to bear the strain. Marsaili's hands flew to her face in horror, unable to either watch or tear her gaze away. His leg twisted and a snap like the crack of a whip sounded in the crystalline air as Lord de Wylde crumpled to the ground.

CHAPTER THIRTEEN

T HROUGH THE FOG of pain, hands appeared, trying to help him up, pulling, tugging, pushing him down into the frigid slush that bit into him like lashes from a metal-studded whip. Rising on his elbows, Geoffrey tried to wave them back, certain—hoping, praying—if he was granted a moment of peace, the pain would go away and he could rise on his own.

"Enough!" he roared. Or at least he thought he did. But the men about him gave no sign of hearing him. Someone rushed up with an armful of furs and wrapped one about his shoulders. Someone else—he thought it was Walter—lifted his torso and slid another fur beneath him.

Hours—or perhaps moments—later, an open cart appeared and amid a measured chant from the men surrounding him, he was raised from the ground and placed in the wagon, padding his leg with more furs. Despite the men's care, the movements of his leg sent shards of pain ripping through him. Geoffrey gave a shout and saw and felt no more.

MARSAILI PACED THE floor in the private room, the chill in her veins not one that could be conquered by the fire blazing on the hearth. Her heart still beat painfully in reaction to witnessing Lord de Wyldes's fall, and she drew in deep breaths to ease the tightness in her chest. She cast a glance at the man on the bed, though too many others clustered about him and she could see little except betwixt elbows and hips.

'Tis not *like Andrew! 'Tis* not! But the stench of blood filled the air, and the man on the bed did not move.

Something warm shoved against her hand and she jumped, nearly knocking the mug that Walter held out to her to the floor.

"Here, Milady," he said. "'Twill help warm you."

"No, thank ye, Sir Walter," she said, waving her hand in frustration. "Not now."

He hovered near and Marsaili gave her attention to the knight. His eyes, dark with worry, tugged at her heart, and she placed a hand on his forearm. He glanced down at her touch, then met her gaze. 'Twas easy to see the concern in his face, and Marsaili had to appreciate his thoughtfulness at such a time.

She offered a slight smile. "Thank ye. I will hold it to warm my hands, but I truly couldnae keep anything in my stomach, I'm that nervous."

A corner of Walter's mouth turned up in a wry grin and he gave a short nod. "I am no good at this sort of thing. I'd rather face an army of cursed Scots than the pain of a wounded friend."

Marsaili knew the exact moment Walter caught the error of his words. His eyes rounded and his lips parted in a small 'o'.

"I'm sorry, Milady. I spoke without thinking. I beg your pardon."

This time her smile was genuine as she sought to put the knight at ease. "Dinnae fash, Sir Walter. I'm not easy in a sickroom, either, and would rather face a horde of armored knights and their men-at-arms than be forced to attend a *cirurgian*."

Bloody linens landed on the floor near her feet with a sickening splat. Marsaili averted her head and swallowed hard.

"You do not have to remain here, Milady," Walter

said. "It would not do to require the *cirurgian* to attend you next."

Marsaili spared him a grimace, thankful to not embarrass herself by fainting or losing what little remained on her stomach after their meager meal hours earlier. But the thought of leaving Lord de Wylde at such a time filled her with a sense of panic.

"Thank ye, but I will remain. I dinnae want to . . . ." Her voice trailed off, uncertain why she felt her presence ensured a good outcome for Lord de Wylde. It didn't make sense, but she simply knew she could not wait in the hall below for news of his progress.

Walter nodded. "I understand. He must have friends around in case . . . ." He, too, left his sentence unfinished, not voicing the unthinkable. He grabbed a chair from the corner of the room and set it beside her. "Here. At least be as comfortable as you can. I will wait with you."

Marsaili settled stiffly into the cushioned comfort, surprised at how tense her muscles were as they slowly relaxed. "Thank you, Sir Walter. Ye have always had an eye out for me. I owe ye my life, ye know."

Walter shifted his feet. "'Twas not I, but The Saint who brought you back to life," he demurred.

"Nae," she argued. "If ye hadnae found me and carried me inside, I would have frozen to death in that barn." She touched his hand. "Ye mustn't think ye cannae cope with people who are injured. Even if ye only considered it yer duty to assist me, ye dinnae shirk what ye knew was right."

"'Tis afterward I feel as I do," he admitted. "In the midst of battle, I do not see or feel what is happening around me. I perform as I have been taught. 'Tis my vocation and I am a superior swordsman."

Marsaili gave his hand a squeeze. It was clear the man merely spoke the truth, simply and without a hint of arrogance. "And 'tis easy to see ye are a loyal friend as well."

"Here," he said, motioning to those who assisted the healer, "I am as helpless as a babe."

"He'll come through this," she assured him with more confidence than she felt. For she did not know which was worse—a man who screamed beneath the knife of a cirurgian, or one who remained as silent as death.

MARSAILI STARTLED AWAKE at the touch to her

shoulder. Walter stared down at her, his face half-hidden in shadows. Simon appeared next to him and dread swamped Marsaili's stomach.

"The break loosened the metal embedded against the bone in his leg and the *cirurgian* was able to remove it. With God's mercy, The Saint will soon recover." Walter smiled, relief evident on his face.

"Lord de Wylde is fortunate to have our old *cirurgian* attend him. He had been captured by Mamluks during Crusade," Simon added. "As a prisoner, he served under an Arab physician, where he learned many unusual skills. I did not know he had been released and returned from the Holy Land, but his arrival here scarcely a week ago was quite fortuitous."

Marsaili blinked heavily, their words failing to register fully as she struggled with lingering fatigue and despondency. Suddenly, understanding dawned. Her gaze darted immediately to the figure on the bed where Lord de Wylde lay motionless beneath the drape of blankets. Simon gave her a reassuring nod as he helped her to her feet.

"He sleeps. The healer made a potion for him and he was able to drink it an hour or so ago after he awoke briefly. He needs to be out of pain and resting, not arguing with the rest of us about staying abed."

A tired smile played about Marsaili's lips. "He willnae thank ye for drugging him."

Simon winked at her. "We will worry about that later."

Marsaili scrubbed her forehead with her fingertips. "I must have slept hard to have missed everything."

"Like a log," Walter murmured, unable to stop smiling. "Come. I'll escort you to a room where you can refresh yourself. Simon will take this watch."

Walter's light grip on her elbow was welcome as he guided Marsaili to a room at the end of the hallway. The door opened silently on its leather hinges.

"You will be comfortable here, Milady. These were Lady de Wylde's rooms. The Saint's mother. She passed a few months ago. The steward has offered you your choice of clothing from the chests, and water will be up for your bath in a few moments."

"'Twill need to be quick to catch me before I fall asleep again," she sighed, eyeing the large bed in the center of the room with longing. "Please give him my thanks. This is most kind of him."

"I believe he said he was honored to see to the comfort of Lord de Wylde's lady."

Marsaili's gaze cut to Walter, but his face remained impassive—except for a slight crinkle at the outer corner of his eyes.

"Hmmph. Lord de Wylde's *guest*," she corrected. Not waiting for Walter's response, she slipped inside the room and closed the door.

She regarded the spacious room, noting the wall-hangings that warmed the room, and the plush tapestry spread at her feet. 'Twas a most unusual spot for such handiwork, but a bedpost pinned it to the floor, indicating it had been placed there on purpose and had not simply fallen from the wall. Marsaili hiked up her skirts to remove her boots and stockings and stepped onto the fabric. The cool texture of the threads warmed quickly beneath her feet.

Not something to have in the hall where muddy feet would ruin such a beautiful piece of work, but I like it in the bedroom. She spied a thick lambswool fleece beside the bed—exactly where her feet would touch the floor when she rose from her nap. Grinning, she scurried over and stood atop the fluffy pelt, delighting in the softness enveloping her feet.

Realizing someone would soon arrive with water for her bath, she strode to one of the two chests along the wall and opened the lid. An array of soft linens and silks met her gaze. She gently pushed the light fabrics aside, her fingers encountering the plush nap of velvet deeper inside. Lifting the folded cloth, she withdrew a surcoat of rich rust hue, trimmed in gold braid with sparkling topaz crystals sewn in a double row at the neck.

Rising, she draped the gown over the foot of the bed, adding a creamy bliaud of such soft wool she could scarcely keep her fingers from caressing the nap. Setting a silk under-gown atop her finds, she responded to a knock at the door.

A ferocious, high-pitched barking erupted, and a small dog charged into the room from a doorway Marsaili hadn't noticed before. The little red dog, ears pricked excitedly, leapt forward, biting at the base of the panel, bouncing back as the door opened. Back and forth the creature darted, tiny feet scarcely meeting the floor as a red-faced woman bustled inside, a stream of lads carrying buckets of steaming water at her heels.

"Beatrice!" She rapped out the name like a military commander, but the little dog only added a comical wiggle to its antics as she danced excitedly before the woman. Marsaili laughed. Instantly, the dog whirled, bristling. In an instant, Beatrice was at Marsaili's feet, sniffing, barking, sniffing, barking.

"Cease!" the other woman bellowed. Beatrice shot her a wounded look and slipped behind Marsaili's skirts, peering around them cautiously. The woman glared a warning at the dog and, motioning the lads through the doorway the dog had entered, gave Marsaili an apologetic smile.

"I'm sorry, Milady. Beatrice is a handful but means well. She was the dowager's pet and has been pining in her rooms these past months. She is always happy to see me but cannot be persuaded to leave her late mistress's quarters."

Marsaili glanced at the wee dog who was quietly sniffing the muddy hem of her skirt. "Does she bite?"

"Oh, no, Milady, though she won't get close enough for petting if she doesn't like you. She never left Lady de Wylde's side through her illness—old age, really. And here she stays."

Beatrice glanced up, her short muzzle and promi-nent chin giving her a cheeky appearance, her large, wide-set eyes brimming with intelligence. Wiry hair stood out all over her face like a man in desperate need of a shave, her prick ears scarcely visible above the unruly spikes.

Sinking slowly into a crouch, Marsaili held out her hand. "Come here, Beatrice. I willnae hurt ye."

The dog cocked her head to the side but did not approach. She wagged her stumpy tail and turned her attention to the lads who quietly exited the room, empty buckets in hand.

"Give her time, Milady. Once she decides you are a friend, you won't be able to take a step without her." Her hands flew upward. "Oh! What am I thinking? You need out of those stained clothes and into a nice warm bath. I am Margery de Langton, chatelaine here at Belwyck. Please call me Margery. My husband is the steward. I am the person you ask for if you need anything at all."

She bustled forward, turning Marsaili about as she chattered, unlacing her gown with quick fingers. Tossing Marsaili's clothing to the floor, Margery guided her into the next room with a hand between her shoulder blades. A tub filled with steaming water greeted her and Marsaili's knees weakened at the blissful sight.

Margery rummaged on a shelf and poured a measure of dried herbs from a wooden box into the tub.

Aromas of lavender and a hint of mint wafted in the air. Marsaili climbed into the fragrant water, sinking into the heated depths.

Hands splayed on her ample hips, Margery continued. "Do you need assistance? I have time to wash your hair if you'd like. Tomorrow I will find a maid for you, but you'll have to do for yourself this evening."

"I dinnae need a maid, Margery, but if ye have time to help with my hair, it would be welcome."

"Of course you need a maid," the woman replied briskly, pouring a pitcher of water over Marsaili's head. "A lady needs someone to care for her clothes and tend her needs." She scooped a handful of scented soap from another box and lathered Marsaili's hair.

Marsaili sighed as Margery's fingertips massaged her scalp. "Mayhap, but I am only staying until Lord de Wylde is back on his feet and able to arrange for the rest of my journey home."

Margery's fingers stilled and she leaned to the side, drawing even with Marsaili's shoulder. "But, you can't be leaving."

Marsaili blinked. "Why not?"

"Because Lord de Wylde has said you're staying."

CHAPTER FOURTEEN

T HE EDGE OF the tub, though thoughtfully covered with a rolled section of linen to cushion the narrow lip, grew more uncomfortable by the minute. Marsaili sighed.

And the water's cooled off as well. She eyed her wrinkled fingers with a rueful twist of her lips. *I suppose 'tis time to climb out and get to bed.*

She hauled herself stiffly to her feet, grateful for the small brazier nearby that glowed merrily, heating the small room. Reaching for a square of linen to dry herself with, she spied the little dog a few feet away, head on her paws, mournful eyes staring at her.

"Hello, wee one," she murmured, not wanting to frighten the animal away. "Beatrice, isn't it?" When the dog didn't move, Marsaili ventured a step out of the tub. The little terrier lifted its head from its paws and watched as Marsaili dried off, her motions smooth and slow, calculated to not alarm the dog.

"Ye miss Lady de Wylde, aye? Well, I'm not planning on taking her place, but 'twould be nice to be friends whilst I am here."

Beatrice cocked her head to one side and Marsaili decided the dog liked her voice. And she certainly enjoyed the dog's company. "Dinnae listen to Margery—or Lord de Wylde, for that matter," she confided. "I will have a talk with him as soon as he's feeling better. 'Tis likely he simply meant for the steward to accord me a room as a guest and not to turn me out. I would imagine his lordship is finding it difficult to express himself properly around the numbing herbs the healer is dosing him with."

The little terrier sneezed, giving a comical jerk of her head as her nose tapped the floor with the strength of her snort.

"Och! Be careful, lass! 'Tis a hard floor beneath ye."

Beatrice wiggled her stumpy tail, her whole rump joining in. Marsaili laughed and grabbed her clothing.

Settling the silk under gown on her shoulders, Marsaili smoothed it over her hips then reached for the soft bliaud. "I'll just lay down for a wee bit and be on my feet again by the evening meal." She lifted a heavy wool blanket from the seat of a chair as she entered the bedroom. Climbing atop the massive bed, she dragged the cover to her shoulders and burrowed into the soft mattress with a sigh.

Light taps across the blanket announced Beatrice's presence on the bed. Marsaili smiled as the little dog circled thrice, bunching up a bit of the cover beneath her feet. She collapsed onto the spot and curled against Marsaili's leg, tucking her nose to her side. Within moments, Beatrice was sound asleep, and Marsaili drifted off into a deep slumber.

GEOFFREY GRITTED HIS teeth against the pain. "Get that vile potion away from me," he growled, stoutly refusing the noxious liquid the healer shoved under his nose. "Find someone who needs it."

"You will regret your decision, milord," Simon vowed cheerfully as he strode into the room, dismissing the healer with a wave of his hand. The woman snatched up her accoutrements and hurried away.

"Regret letting my mind clear for the first time in three days?" Geoffrey narrowed his eyes. "I suppose you and Walter thought it in my best interest for me to languish here in a fog? Damn it, I've dealt with my injury for nearly a year. I can manage."

Simon collapsed comfortably into the chair next to the bed.

Geoffrey scowled, finding fault yet again. "And put the furniture back as it was. It looks like a sickroom in here."

With a laugh, Simon ignored his liege. "It has been a sickroom for the past few days and will remain so a bit longer. Someone has sat with you continually since your accident. Lady Marsaili would not leave your side except when Walter or I forced her to and promised to remain in her place."

Geoffrey ignored Simon's sidelong glance. With a shrug, the knight continued. "The healer is not responsible for your good fortune—"

"Good fortune?" Geoffrey exploded, motioning to the bed. "You call this good fortune?"

Simon's patient gaze and pitying smile nearly drove Geoffrey to madness.

"Milord, I would be happy to tell you the how of it if you could promise to limit your outbursts during the tale."

Inhaling a deep, steadying breath, Geoffrey settled against the pile of cushions at his back. He waved a hand in the air in mock benevolence. "Proceed."

"When you fell on the ice, you broke your leg."

Geoffrey opened his mouth, but clamped it shut again at Simon's lifted brow.

"The break loosened the metal piece wedged against the bone." Simon waved Geoffrey's burgeoning protest aside. "Here is the best part. Our *cirurgian*, captured several years ago in the Holy Land whilst on Crusade, has returned. Not only has he honed his skills on a very fertile battlefield, but learned some interesting procedures from an Arab physician whilst a prisoner."

Geoffrey stilled, listening intently, almost afraid to ask what had been done. His head still felt as though it was packed with lint, but a sharp note of warning chased it away, bringing clarity and the recognition Simon could be right. He may soon regret turning the healer's potion away.

Simon stood and flipped back the light wool covering from Geoffrey's leg. To his relief, Geoffrey saw both legs, though one was encased between two stout planks of wood and bound with strips of linen.

"He felt the crossbow tip beneath his fingers as he assessed the break," Simon continued. "After some discussion, he took the liberty of divesting you of that pesky reminder of Godfrey's poor marksmanship." He pulled the blanket back into place and reached for a small bowl on the table next to the bed. Plucking a twisted piece of metal from the container, he held it up for Geoffrey's inspection.

"I don't suppose you want to keep this, but I wished to show it to you."

"He cut open my leg?" Geoffrey asked, his voice surprisingly hoarse. It was largely unheard of, though he'd known of battlefield *cirurgians* taking immense gambles with treatment of horrific injuries. Most did little to prolong the life of the victim.

Simon nodded. "Aye. A bit of surgery he seemed quite adept with. 'Tis a small hole, really. Not much larger than this." He turned the tip back and forth in the sun's glow, but the dull black surface simply absorbed the light.

"Such a small thing to have caused you such an inconvenience. Had the *cirurgian* been here when you were first injured, he could have saved you a year's suffering."

A thought fisted in Geoffrey's stomach. "And possibly saved my brothers' lives as well had I been here to protect them."

Simon shook his head as he tossed the metal back to the bowl. "Your brothers lived by their own codes. 'Twas rare they heeded your advice before Robert became lord. There is no guarantee your presence would have changed how they lived their lives after your father's control over them passed." He captured Geoffrey's gaze. "And 'tis a sin to assume you could change God's plan for them."

Geoffrey closed his eyes. "You are right, Simon. I must see the *cirurgian* is thanked properly."

"He says as soon as your wound heals, you may begin taking a few steps about your bedroom, gaining a bit more strength each day."

Geoffrey winced and glared at Simon. "How long does he think I'm to wear this infernal contraption?"

With a laugh, Simon patted Geoffrey's shoulder and turned to the door. "I will let him explain. Is there anything you wish me to get for you?"

"Crutches."

THE SHRILL SOUND of a woman's voice intruded on his thoughts. Mayhap 'twas best he set aside his consideration to have either Simon or the *cirurgian* killed—or at least banished from his sight for the foreseeable future. The *cirurgian* denied his request to get out of bed, and Simon—blast his eyes—backed the man up. Most emphatically.

The woman's voice grew louder and, to Geoffrey's dismay, the portal opened, admitting Marsaili and an entourage he would have sworn was loyal to him.

Until today.

Simon held the door open while Marsaili swept into the room. Walter stepped around her and pulled the chair back to the bedside from the hearth where Geoffrey had banished it only a few hours earlier. The *cirurgian* followed on her heels. A dark red blur dashed across the room, barking wildly as it hurled itself upon the bed.

"Ouch!" Geoffrey complained, trying to capture the small beast as she leapt about, sneaking wet doggy kisses between his futile attempts to stop her.

"Beatrice!" Marsaili scolded mildly. "Ladies dinnae leap into men's beds and proceed to lick them to death." She snapped her fingers and pointed to the floor, but Beatrice ignored the command, compromising with a seat to Geoffrey's right, out of Marsaili's reach.

Geoffrey immediately tensed as his body stiffened in response to Marsaili's unintentional innuendo. At least he hoped it was unintentional. He'd been convalescing just fine, managing to make it through the day with few thoughts of her and the kisses they'd shared. That those few thoughts generally lasted an hour or so at a time was entirely irrelevant. Now she'd added further fodder for his torment, and he was beginning to wish he'd given Simon the job of arranging escort for her to return home.

But he couldn't escape a nagging feeling she still needed protection beyond what an armed chaperone could provide. And now he needed a distraction from the image of her tumbling into his bed and licking him into pleasurable release. He groaned.

"How are ye feeling, milord?" Marsaili's smile was bright as she stood by his bed, ignoring the chair. She placed a palm on his arm and his skin burst into flames, scorching its way to a portion of his anatomy he'd only just gotten under control. "The *cirurgian* tells me ye dinnae wish to stay abed."

Geoffrey thought he detected a playful note to her voice, but he chose to not answer her accusation. No sense arguing over something he would do in the next day or two with or without her blessing. He caressed the dog's head, causing her to wiggle excitedly. "I see you and Beatrice have become friends."

His words had the desired distracting effect as Marsaili's gaze swept from him to the dog whose bristly face stared adoringly at him.

"Yer steward gave me Lady de Wylde's rooms. I hope 'tis not a problem. I dinnae imagine ye were in yer right mind when ye first arrived. If I need to move, I can."

"No. I told him to put you in my mother's rooms. I believe I had a lucid moment or two. I'm glad Beatrice likes you."

"Margery told me she's pined for yer ma something terrible and hasnae left her rooms since . . . ." Marsaili's voice trailed off uncertainly. Her clear eyes clouded.

Geoffrey gave her a gentle smile. "Don't worry. She was an incredible woman, but her years at last caught up with her. Her children came to her long after she thought she'd be blessed with them. 'Twas sorrowful to hear she'd passed, but not entirely unexpected."

The *cirurgian* stepped forward and moved the blanket aside to expose Geoffrey's leg. Marsaili's face paled and she took a quick step back. Geoffrey clamped a hand over his groin to keep the covering in place, hiding his waning erection from view. No one seemed to pay him the slightest attention, however, their gazes glued to the *cirurgian's* work as he unwound the bandage.

As his body eased, Geoffrey turned his interest to seeing the wound for the first time. To his surprise, it was little more than a small nick in his leg, closed by several neatly placed black stitches. The *cirurgian* prodded the area lightly with his fingertips.

"Any pain, milord?" he asked.

Geoffrey denied the ache, loathe to admit to an illness when there was so much he needed to be doing. And damned if he'd admit to a little pain in front of his knights. Or Marsaili.

"You poke a wound and ask if there's pain?" He gave the man a wry grin and shooed him away. "I am forever in your debt. Be assured of your place here always. Is there anything you desire?"

"It is my desire to teach my skills to others, milord. If you would allow a few apprentices, I would be grateful."

"With my heartfelt appreciation and my funding. It

is yours. Anything else?"

The man beamed. "If you could be persuaded to drink this potion, milord . . . ."

CHAPTER FIFTEEN

MARSAILI HID A grin at the rebellious glare Lord de Wylde leveled at the *cirurgian*.

Milord's saintly attitude extends to granting a seat of learning to the man, but not so far as to abiding by his potions and advice. She gave in to the merriment and laughed. Lorde de Wylde shot her a quelling look.

"Come along, Beatrice," she called in a sing-song voice as she scooped the dog into her arms. The little terrier, quite used to Marsaili after three days of petting and blatant use of bribery, nestled in Marsaili's arms, giving her chin a quick lick to demonstrate her approval.

Marsaili wiped the damp spot away. "We should leave his lordship to discuss his progress with the *cirurgian* without our ogling his nether limbs."

"Wait," Lord de Wylde commanded. He encompassed the remainder of the group in one sweeping glance. "Leave us."

The room cleared with remarkable speed. Marsaili primly took the seat Walter had acquired for her. "I would like to say I'm glad ye are doing so well. I thought my heart had stopped when ye fell on the ice."

"Simon tells me you've become rather attached to that chair," Lord de Wylde noted with a nod to where she sat.

Her cheeks heated. "Sir Simon talks too much," she murmured. Stroking the dog's furry head, she stalled for time to gather her thoughts. The merest idea she could care for the stern man who surprised and warmed her with the passion of his kisses pushed all reasonable thinking from her mind.

"Ye have been verra kind to me," she finally allowed.

His voice dropped low, seductive. "Even though I—"

Marsaili interrupted him with a jerk of her chin, determined to keep from addressing the attraction between them. "Aye, even though ye disregarded my wishes and slowed me down with yer need to protect me." She leaned forward and Beatrice leapt the small space to the bed where she curled up at Lord de Wylde's side.

"Which brings up the next point—I would appreciate verra much if ye would appoint a guard for me so I can continue to the border. I willnae require yer men to cross into Scotland. Once there, they may turn back, for I will then be quite safe."

Lord de Wylde's gaze narrowed. "You are safe here," he stated. "I believe Lord de Ville will continue his attempts to seize you until he is certain you are out of his reach. 'Tis a three day ride to Lockardebi from here in good weather, and that offers too much opportunity for his henchmen."

"Which is why ye offered to send a guard with me," Marsaili rapped out, her temper to the snapping point. "A few knights should deter even the most fool-hardy scoundrels."

"But not those with the promise of excellent payment once you're turned over to your Edmund," Geoffrey countered.

"He's not *my* Edmund!" she exploded, slamming her palms on the chair's armrests. "I dinnae wish to remain here."

"It will be easier to protect you—temporarily," he amended as she bristled. "—from here. On the road, in this weather, you are too exposed."

"Ye promised!" Marsaili's voice rose and she

choked back tears of frustration.

"I promised to protect you. And I will. 'Twill only be for a short time."

"How long?" she asked, dragging the words out grudgingly.

Something flashed in Lord de Wylde's eyes, but she could not put a name to it. Her heart doubled its beat and she sent fervent thanks to God for putting Geoffrey in bed with a broken leg. 'Twould be easier to avoid the man whilst she cooled her heels in his castle.

"Mayhap a few weeks," he replied. "Until the weather breaks."

Marsaili sank back into the chair with a deep sigh. "I wish . . . ." Her voice trailed off.

"What do you wish, milady?"

She sent him a crushing glare. "I wish ye'd taken the damn potion."

⟫⟫⟫⟫⟫⟪⟪⟪⟪

MARSAILI STARED AT the falling snow in exasperation, impatiently tapping her toe on the wooden floor. "Of course the bad weather would begin again."

The comment brought no response from the little dog who lay contentedly by the hearth, chewing enthusiastically on a bone.

Wincing at the blast of icy air blowing through the open window, Marsaili slammed the heavy shutters closed, flipping the latch to keep the panels in place.

Beatrice stopped her gnawing, snapping her head up to stare at Marsaili as she flounced over to the bed. With a reluctant look at her bone, the dog abandoned it for the prospect of a good cuddle, landing beside Marsaili on the mattress in a single, effortless bound.

Marsaili ruffled the animal's ears. "I could have gone on my own, Beatrice. It has been two weeks and his lordship is bed-ridden and cannae stop me." She waved her hands in the air dramatically. "But this . . . this . . . ." She sighed.

"Why should I be forced to stay here with *him*? And dinnae tell me he is bed-ridden and therefore of no threat to me," she warned the dog. "Every day I am compelled to visit, to laugh at something Sir Simon says as they joke about."

She turned on her side, her voice dropping to a whisper. "I love his smile, Beatrice. I would turn myself inside out to make him laugh. To see his eyes light up. Did ye know he has wee dimples on his cheeks when he smiles? I suppose 'tis not manly for it to be mentioned, but I have noticed."

Marsaili rolled to her back, staring at the draperies overhead. "I must leave, Beatrice. He has bewitched me. I am no starry-eyed lass dreaming of things that cannae be. He willnae take a Scottish woman to wife, and I wouldnae want a warrior English husband if he offered. His leg will now heal and he will be whole once again."

She sighed. "Being a border lord means he will be forced to go to war from time-to-time. 'Tis simply the way of things. Though I dinnae love my scholarly husband, I suppose we got along well enough. Except for Edmund's interference, things werenae so bad. We saw little of each other and dinnae live in fear for our lives."

Beatrice cocked her funny face, ears barely poking above the bristly fur.

"I suppose ye think me foolish for thinking I can make it home on my own," Marsaili huffed. "I am quite an accomplished rider, and my skills with a dagger were drilled into me by my elder brother from the time I could heft the blade. Ma would have skinned us alive had she known, but I managed to hide the little nicks and cuts fairly well. It dinnae take me long to learn, and I've not done myself damage since."

She sighed again. "I will simply have to think of another plan. I dinnae believe my self-respect would survive if his lordship kissed me again."

And the possibility she would succumb to the temptation to kiss Lord de Wylde if she lingered much longer in his presence was something she was unwilling to admit, even to Beatrice.

GEOFFREY MULLED OVER Walter's report. He sat before the hearth, right leg stretched to the warmth of the blaze. After two weeks flat on his back, this past fortnight had seen grudging improvement as the cirurgian had allowed an infuriatingly slow return to normalcy. Heat reduced the soreness in his muscles that had seen too little exercise of late.

"You gave orders her horse was not to be released except upon your direct approval?" Geoffrey leveled his gaze at the knight.

Walter nodded. "Aye. The stable master said she'd visited her horse often these past few days, asking him where the tack was kept, wanting to check for possible damage done to the girths by the cold, wet weather."

"A plausible request. But I doubt milady had only the condition of her tack in mind."

"'Tis what I thought, as well. I reiterated your order, and he readily agreed."

Geoffrey remained silent for a moment. Reaching a decision, he tossed aside the blanket across his lap. "Hand me those crutches. I need exercise."

Walter held the wooden props as Geoffrey waved aside his offer of assistance rising from the chair. With a nod of satisfaction, Geoffrey noted the twinge in his leg had become negligible, and his muscles reacted firmly, smoothing the limp from his gait. He took a few slow steps, testing the strength of his leg.

"Just one of them," he said, reaching for the crutch. By using it in tandem with his injured leg, he found he could maneuver rather well, provided he did not rush. Triumph surged over him. "Have a new cane made. I will not use this crutch beyond today."

Grinning, Walter loped toward the door. "Aye, milord. You will have a cane tonight if I have to make it myself."

The door closed behind Walter. Geoffrey stood in the center of the room, feet braced shoulder-width apart, his body responding to the muscle-memory of exercises long put aside. Though the splint restricted much of the movements of his legs, he hefted his sword, working his upper body from a stationary position. A fine sheen of sweat formed on his brow and between his shoulder blades, but he relished the return to action.

I've remained inactive too long. Between the cirurgian's dire warnings should I over-stress the leg and Marsaili's clucking like a mother hen, I have had little opportunity to move about. Slow and easy. Push only to the point of pain—a step beyond—relax.

He rested, breathing deeply but not too hard. Pleased, he flexed his hand on the grip of his sword. It felt good. Damn good.

I am Lord de Wylde. 'Tis time I reclaimed my place.

At the evening meal, the chatter in the hall fell to silence as Lord de Wylde clattered slowly down the stone staircase, Walter's burly frame a step or two ahead. Geoffrey's gaze swept the room, noting Simon's nod of approval as well as Marsaili's pallor. Walter crossed to the head table, pulling out the heavy chair. Geoffrey approached with measured tread, the crutch bearing most of his weight on his right side. He'd badgered the *cirurgian* to reduce the splint to something he could manage, but it still mandated a careful gait.

He lowered himself to the seat, extending his right leg beneath the table. It ached, but the sense of accomplishment overrode the discomfort.

"Please continue," he said, facial muscles straining with the effort to suppress his grin, amazed at how good it felt to be among the people again.

A shout went up about the room as the castle inhabitants cheered. The din quickly deafened as they pounded the tables, their booted feet stomping the stone floor. Geoffrey inclined his head in acknowledgement, signaling a serving wench for his trencher. When it became clear he expected no further notice to be taken of his return, the meal was quickly resumed.

Marsaili, seated on Simon's right, leaned forward. "Ye took a chance coming down those stairs, milord," she chided, disapproval twisting her lips.

"Walter was there to catch me," Geoffrey demurred, dismissing her censure. He accorded her a small smile. "I cannot remain ensconced above stairs. My muscles and joints stiffen more each day. I have promised the *cirurgian* I will not act unduly and he has agreed a moderate increase in my exercise is appropriate."

"I dinnae suppose ye gave him a choice," Marsaili tossed at him, the worry in her eyes betraying her concern.

Geoffrey sent her a wolfish grin. "Not a one."

Marsaili leaned back in her chair and resumed cutting the meat on her trencher. "I was speaking with Simon before ye arrived. The weather has warmed and the snow is beginning to melt. 'Twill be spring soon, and I believe 'tis time for me to continue my journey home."

Her words, though spoken quietly, did not settle well. Even with her daily visits well-chaperoned—which he was certain she arranged—he had grown accustomed to her presence. But he had to agree there was little reason to keep her at Belwyck much longer. Once the snows melted completely, the roads would be clogged with mud. Her window of time to leave was fast approaching.

Unless he made her an offer. Since their encounter in the wagon, he'd had no indication from her if she would welcome his advances. Not that he had been in any condition to make them.

She is so very lovely. Her spirit inspires me and her

beauty touches me in a way no other has. Life with Lady Marsaili would never be dull, but it would be passionate and it would be fascinating. I admire her courage and her honor, and 'tis apparent she has made herself at home here. The people have accepted her and my knights dote on her.

Perhaps he could stall a few days more. If he had some indication their attraction had not been a passing thing and she'd grown weary of him in the past weeks. He smiled, determined to let her know he would welcome her thoughts later—in private.

"Milady, might we—"

The door to the hall opened, interrupting his words. A soldier bustled in, angling for Simon. "Sir—" Catching sight of Lord de Wylde, the man checked and bowed low.

"Milord, a group of men approached the gates. The leader wishes to speak with you. What do you command?"

"State his name and business."

"Lord Edmund de Ville. He declares you harbor a wanted criminal in the castle."

CHAPTER SIXTEEN

MARSAILI'S HEART STOPPED. She gripped the knife she held in her fist tight, her fingernails biting into her palm. Chills bristled the hairs along her arms, filling her skin with the buzzing sensation of danger. Her vision dimmed.

"Put Lord de Ville in my solar. His men can cool their heels outside the gates," Geoffrey rapped, his voice hard. His gaze slammed into Marsaili's and she gasped with sudden insight.

"'Tis what ye waited for!" Her heart regained its beat with a vengeance, tripling its pace, creating a roaring in her ears. Marsaili fought through the fog of disbelief that threatened to paralyze her.

"Ye held me here, waiting for Edmund to attend ye!" She leapt from her chair, her arms and legs trembling. "Ye bastard!"

She fled the room as shouts rose, piling about her head, urging her to greater speed. Snagging the corner post in one hand, she whirled about, flinging herself down the back corridor to the kitchens. Her skirts whipped about her legs and she reached low and grabbed the heavy fabric, hoisting it above her knees as she freed her legs to a faster pace.

The kitchen was ablaze with warmth from the cooking hearths and the chatter of the women who busied themselves with preparing the meal. A young lad tended the pig carcass roasting over a low fire while another carved slices onto a platter. Marsaili entered the room at a sedate pace, her pulse racing. She smiled briefly at a couple of women who sent her curious looks, and they quickly returned to their duties.

Slipping out the back door, she plucked a cloak from a hook near the entry, its fabric stained and faded, creating a dappled appearance that lent excellent cover in the gloaming. Behind her, voices rose excitedly and she knew she remained only a few steps ahead of Lord de Wylde's men. She bolted across the yard, keeping to the lengthening shadows as much as possible, skirting the outbuildings until she reached the edge of the stable. Lounging against the stone wall, a stable boy idly held the reins of a blood bay horse with tall white stockings, its blanketed covering blue, edged in a wide golden border.

Edmund!

She'd recognize his horse and trappings anywhere. Marsaili flattened herself against the side of the building, thinking furiously. This time of day, her horse would be fed and stabled for the night. The last time she'd visited Hew, the stable master had watched her closely. Lord de Wylde's men would undoubtedly expect her to flee on her own horse. She eyed the bay who nibbled lazily at his reins.

They would not expect her to take Edmund's horse.

On silent feet, Marsaili slid to the far door to the stable and entered, noting with alarm the knight who already stood watch at Hew's stall. Keeping to the shadows, Marsaili slipped into the room the stable boys shared, lifting a tunic, pair of breeches and short coat from various hooks. Aware the lads were eating dinner at a low table in the hall, she quickly stripped out of her gown, pulling on the rough breeches and shirt. Leaving her braid trapped beneath the tunic, she shrugged her shoulders forward, letting the drape of the coat hide the bulge of her breasts.

She shoved her gown and surcoat behind a pile of straw and strolled nonchalantly down the hall of the darkened barn as she yanked a knitted cap over her head, too intent on escape to worry about what vermin likely nested in the woolen strands. She shuffled through the front door and approached the lad holding the horse.

"Go get yer food." She wiped her nose on her sleeve with a loud sniff and slid one hand around to her backside, giving it a vigorous scratch. "I'm new and get the worst jobs," she added, disgust in her voice. "Does he bite?"

The lad's stomach rumbled loudly. He straightened from his post against the wall and handed her the reins. "Naw, but he kicks somethin' fierce."

"Damn beast," Marsaili muttered, flipping the leather strips to make the horse toss his head. The lad's laughter quickly disappeared as he scurried away to his dinner.

The instant she lost sight of the lad, Marsaili stripped the saddle and blanket from the horse's back. *Damn! He still looks good.* Pulling her dagger from the sheath at her leg, she hacked at the horse's mane until silky black strands lay in a pile at her feet. Doing a similar service to the horse's tail, she kicked the shorn hair beneath some hay scattered a few feet away. For once glad of the results of the melting snow, she scooped some mud in her hands and smeared it on the horse's legs, dimming the brilliant white stockings, then added a smudge to her face to complete their disguise.

With a quick hop, she managed to land on her stomach atop the horse's back. She wiggled into a seated position and draped the worn cloak about her and the horse. Slouching, she urged the beast to a walk. Tired from his long journey, the horse plodded along, and Marsaili joined a few straggling peasants leaving through the castle gates. Guiding the horse down the middle of the road leading to the village, Marsaili garnered scant notice from the guards at the gate. From the corner of her eye, she saw Edmund's band of soldiers, their banner flipping idly in the evening breeze.

She clenched her hands on the reins, quelling the urge to spur the horse into a run, holding back the fear and anger. She refused to think about Lord de Wylde's betrayal, knowing it would rob her of the ability to think straight. And right now, her very life depended on clear thoughts and precise planning.

To lessen her chances of attracting attention, she

dismounted, leaving the cloak bunched across the horse's back, and trudged toward the village, weary horse trailing behind her. People passed them, but likely anticipating a hot meal and an early bed, none spoke to her or gave her more than a glance.

Thundering hooves approached from behind and Marsaili shuffled quickly to the side of the road, her body tense with apprehension. Four knights, their armor glinting in the moonlight, rumbled past. A grin edged across her face. They were still looking for Lady Marsaili, not a woman dressed as a stable boy.

To give them a trail to follow should they realize their mistake, she continued along the road through the village. Drawing even with the blacksmith's forge, she walked the bay through the mud, mingling his hoof prints with those already on the churned ground. Then, avoiding the softer ground as much as possible, she dodged the fenced area behind the small barn and led the horse deep into the forest.

GEOFFREY FLUNG HIS cane across the room and sank into his chair. "Tell me you did not lose a vocal, angry woman. Tell me you did NOT let her slip past the guard at the gate. TELL ME she is under guard in her room, awaiting my questions." His voice rose to a roar, but he didn't care.

"Damn!" He slammed his fist down on the arm of the chair, ignoring the shock that raced up his arm at the force of the blow.

Simon waited the space of a heartbeat before speaking. "The men have not yet returned from their search of the village. 'Tis dark—"

"I know 'tis dark!" Geoffrey snapped. "Send others out at first light. I do not want her getting away."

"You believe her guilty?" Simon asked, surprise in his voice.

"No!" Geoffrey lowered his voice. "Though I haven't spoken with Lord de Ville nor read the writ I requested of him."

"Do you suppose he actually has one?"

Geoffrey leveled a harsh look at the knight. "'Twould be foolish of him to waste my time."

A tap sounded at the door. At a nod from Geoffrey, Simon opened the panel. The steward stood there, making no move to enter the room. Geoffrey's estimation of the man's intelligence increased slightly.

"Milord, Lord de Ville still awaits in your solar and

grows restless."

"He can grow roots as far as I am concerned. Until I speak with Lady Marsaili, I do not wish to hear from him."

"Very good, Milord. Shall I have him rest here the night, or suggest he return to his camp and await your summons?"

"Keep him here. He will get into less mischief isolated from his men."

De Langton bowed deeply and hurried away. Simon closed the door.

"You cannot keep him waiting forever, Saint."

Geoffrey quirked his brow. "Then find Marsaili."

⤙⤙⤙ ⤚⤚⤚

MARSAILI HUDDLED AGAINST the horse's side, her face pressed against his shaggy shoulder. She pulled her cloak about her more closely and prayed her feet would not freeze.

'Tis a good thing I preferred my short boots to the slippers in Lady de Wylde's belongings. But I would pay dearly for a set of woolen stockings right now. I've become too used to life inside Belwyck's sturdy walls. Too accustomed to basking in Lord de Wylde's smiles

instead of seeing his true intent.

Her body shook. She tried to tell herself the reaction was from the cold, now that night had fallen, but it was a reflection of the dead spot inside her to realize he'd merely played a waiting game with her. A spot filled with unforgiving heartbreak and misery.

Though I suppose he dinnae break his leg simply so I'd feel sorry for him. She shuddered harder to remember their passionate embrace—and what it could have led to had Lord de Wylde needed a ploy other than her sympathy and kindness to keep her at Belwyck until Edmund arrived.

She clenched her fists. *Damn him! He isnae a saint, but a devil, preying upon those weaker than him. How he must have laughed as I attended his bedside, allowing him to direct my future.* She gritted her teeth, her self-pity dissipating beneath growing anger.

"He willnae control me again," she firmly addressed the horse. "'Tis a hard day's ride to the Border if I dinnae stop." She patted the animal's shoulder. "Ye've been a good beast and I will push ye as hard as ye can go. But I won't be safe until I am home. I can promise ye a bucket of oats and a warm stall once we're there."

Marsaili glanced at the sky. The pale, slivered moon cast little light on the ground. "I hope ye are rested. We're going to ride through the night." The horse gave a snort as Marsaili mounted but did not fight the bit as she urged him forward.

Mountains loomed to her right as a dark stain against the night sky. "We dinnae need to go there," she informed the horse. "I cannae think of a thing I'd rather avoid than a climb into the mountains." A furry ear twitched in her direction. "I dinnae suppose ye're looking for a hike through the hills, either." Marsaili sighed. "I wish I remembered more of my journey into England five years ago. 'Twould help me know which way to go. As soon as 'tis light, I can be sure we're headed north."

They plodded forward, the horse's easy gait lulling Marsaili. The consuming fright and anger faded, leaving exhaustion behind. She weaved side-to-side atop the horse's broad, shaggy back. Pulling the animal to a stop, Marsaili dismounted and stomped her feet, wincing at the tingle in her toes. Deciding to keep active in order to help stay warm, she walked beside the horse.

Morning broke at last as a thin pale line of gray

above the horizon. Marsaili's spirits soared, anticipating the warmth of the day as winter faded into spring. She struggled atop the horse's back again and kept the rising sun on her right. The dark glassy surface of a lake drew her to the water's edge for a drink. The horse pawed the thin film of ice, then drank his fill.

Marsaili let him rest, staring at the path before her to take her mind off her stomach's need for food. "If we can keep going, we'll be home in a day or so." She took a deep breath, savoring the heady expectation. Giving the horse a pat, she prepared to mount.

"I will be free in Scotland," she assured him. "Beyond the reach of both Geoffrey and Edmund."

Aiming for a low ridge, she sought to put the miles between Belwyck and Lokardebi behind her, drumming her heels on the horse's sides as morning light flashed off metal on the hill behind her.

CHAPTER SEVENTEEN

GEOFFREY ENTERED HIS solar, his pace unhurried, hiding the hitch in his gait. Simon followed a mere step behind. Inside the room, a bulky man, his tunic rumpled and untied at the neck, bolted to his feet.

"You cannot keep me here as a prisoner!" he snarled. "I demand you release me at once."

With no more reaction than a raised brow in admonition, Geoffrey continued his path to the desk near the window. He sat, then clasped his hands on the desk's surface, turning his attention to the irate Lord de Ville. Simon stood a pace behind Geoffrey's chair, unobtrusive, yet alert.

"You are, of course, free to go." Geoffrey gestured to the door. Edmund glanced from Lord de Wylde to the door and back. He took a step toward the closed portal. Geoffrey leaned back in his chair, stretching his right leg beneath the desk to ease a sudden cramp.

"You will not be accorded entrance to Belwyck again." He hoped the man was idiot enough to leave.

Edmund returned to his seat.

An insolent grin creased his face. "I will leave as soon as you hand the wench over to me."

Geoffrey sighed. "I fear I cannot do that."

Edmund's leer broadened. He reached inside his cloak, thrown casually across the back of his chair. Geoffrey followed his actions closely. The man withdrew a rolled parchment. "I believe you told my man I was to bring a writ from the king." He offered it to Geoffrey. "'Tis a bit damp." He shrugged. "The weather was unkind."

Geoffrey stared at Edmund's hand for a moment before leaning forward to accept the scroll. Trepidation skittered through his bowels as he anticipated the writing within.

What have you done, Marsaili? We could have worked through this together. Why did you doubt me?

Breaking the wax seal with a flick of a finger, he unrolled the parchment, scanning the poorly scribed and water-marked contents.

By letter wryten as sworn this day . . . and at the

bidding and commaundment of King Henry
III . . . of England . . .

Thys proclement to release Lady (Dowager)
Marsaili de Ville into the custody of Lord
Edmund de Ville . . .

For the purpose of standing trial for the murder
of the late Andrew de Ville . . .

Signed this day . . .

Henry III

By the Grace of God, King of England, Lord of
Ireland, and Duke of Aquitane

With a shake to still his trembling hand, Geoffrey placed the parchment carelessly on his desk. He would have liked nothing better than to drive his fist into Edmund's mocking face. Silence lengthened between them.

"She is not here."

Edmund bounded to his feet. "You defy the king's order?"

Simon rose onto the balls of his feet, his weight tipped forward, poised should Edmund be foolish enough to raise a hand in anger. Geoffrey's level stare belied his simmering temper.

"I was under no orders to detain her."

"My man told you—" Edmund blustered.

Geoffrey waved a hand in the air for silence. "He gave me some garbled story of returning her to Bellevue. As her husband is dead, she has the right to choose where she lives, and she wishes to live in Scotland."

"You had no right to let her go! Furthermore, I have been stuck here for the past two days, and you . . . you . . . you *knew*!" Edmund's face darkened alarmingly.

"I have been inconvenienced of late." Geoffrey shrugged. "My steward has kept you fed?"

Edmund whirled about, muttering under his breath. Geoffrey waited until the man gained control of himself, then continued.

"As soon as you and your men are rested, I ask that you vacate my lands. I care not where you go, but I do not want reports of you lingering beyond the morn. Do I make myself clear?"

Edmund's murderous gaze met his. "Very clear, milord. We will leave at first light."

Geoffrey nodded to Simon and the knight crossed

the room to open the door. "I suggest you inform your men of your plans. They await you outside the gates."

Edmund snatched his cloak and tossed it about his shoulders as he stomped from the room. "You haven't heard the last of this!" he proclaimed. "I will have her!"

Geoffrey gave no answer as Edmund stormed down the hall. A pair of guards fell into step behind him, escorting him from the castle.

"You lied to him," Simon murmured.

"She is not at Belwyck," Geoffrey pointed out.

"You could have told him she is but two days's ride from here."

Geoffrey scowled. "I do not like the man."

"He now has the king involved. In case that gives you pause."

Geoffrey tossed the rolled parchment to Simon. "It is not the king's signature."

⇒⟫⟫⟫⟨⟨⟨⟨⇐

GEOFFREY WATCHED FROM the steps of the great hall as Edmund joined his men beyond the gates. His attention was drawn further afield as four mud-encrusted knights rumbled up the road into Belwyck. The setting sun glinted off the scant areas of armor not covered in dried muck. In their midst trotted a rangy blood-bay horse, his mane and tail in tatters, his coat besmeared with filth. His rider, a slim lad in a faded cloak, sat upright on the horse's bare back.

Damn! Geoffrey glanced sharply through the gate at the riders, then to Edmund's camp. Two men rose from their cook fire and strode to the side of the road.

"That's my horse!" Edmund shouted. "I want that boy hanged!"

"Get her in here now!" Geoffrey ordered. Walter and Simon, already in motion, quickened their step.

"Close the gates!" Simon commanded as the riders swept through the barbican. Chains rattled as the portcullis dropped. Shouts rang out from Edmund's camp.

"It's my horse! I demand justice!" His fists gripped the iron bars as he stared at the retreating riders. He shoved away with a curse, shaking his fist in the air.

Geoffrey ignored him. Every ounce of his being was centered on not murdering the young woman before him. She slid from the horse's back, her knees buckling before she righted. Geoffrey stared at her, making no move to lend her support. Marsaili lifted her chin, strain etched across her muddy face, her eyes defiant.

"Get inside," Geoffrey bit out, not trusting himself to say anything further.

Shoulders back, she stalked past him into the hall. Geoffrey signaled to a servant. "Bring water for her bath."

He followed Marsaili up the stairs and into the rooms she'd vacated two days earlier. Hitching along, leaning heavily on his cane, he disregarded the ache in his leg. He slammed the door closed and Marsaili whirled, fear flaring for an instant in her eyes. Beatrice darted across the floor, barking happily, dancing about on her hind legs, seeking attention. Marsaili gave the dog's head a pat then faced Lord de Wylde.

"What are ye doing?" she demanded.

"You need a good dunking and I need answers to a few questions."

She propped her fists on her hips. "Not whilst I bathe, milord. I will speak with ye when I am finished. Leave the room, please."

"And let you out of my sight again?" Geoffrey queried, shaking his head. "I have no wish to chase you down again."

"Ye? Chase me down?" Marsaili swept him with a derisive gaze. "Ye couldnae chase down a tethered sheep."

"Do you try my patience further?" he asked, astonished at her baiting.

A tap at the door silenced their animosity. "Enter," Geoffrey snapped, moving away from the door as four lads hurried in with buckets of steaming water. Beatrice harried their heels as they emptied the containers into the tub and departed in haste. Geoffrey pushed the door closed.

Marsaili struggled to maintain her composure. She was tired to the very marrow of her bones, and in no condition to do battle with Lord de Wylde. A faint aroma of lavender wafted from the tub, legacy of other baths, beckoning her. She ached all over, including her heart.

I was so close! I could have lived my life never seeing him again and would have been content.

But would she? His betrayal cut deeply, but he'd dragged her upstairs to a bath, not flung her to Edmund and his soldiers. A bath!

Geoffrey scraped a chair from the hearth to the doorway to the bathing chamber, angling it just enough to provide her a modicum of privacy. And no chance for escape.

"Be quick."

Certain he settled into the chair, Marsaili entered the small room and peeled off her grimy clothes. She kicked them to the side and grabbed a handful of dried lavender as she stepped into the tub. Comfort enveloped her, as paralyzing as physical restraints, and she surrendered to the caress of the water.

She quickly soaped her hair, then set about scrubbing her skin, removing the embedded mud and stench.

"You rode due north." It was a statement from Lord de Wylde, not a question, and Marsaili sighed.

"Aye. And mayhap a bit west. I dinnae know the bogs were so deep. Or so . . . boggy."

"They are dangerous if you are not exceedingly careful. I am glad my men were able to get you out."

Marsaili rolled a square of linen for a cushion, then leaned her head against the rim of the tub. Closing her eyes, she wondered how long he would let her soak before he demanded answers to his questions. Would he then turn her over to Edmund? Would his sense of right and wrong deny her justice?

Her eyes watered, and she wiped angrily at them as helplessness rippled through her.

"Tell me, Marsaili," Geoffrey began. "Is this a ploy from Edmund to take you? Or are you guilty of murdering your husband?"

Marsaili turned, staring at him over the edge of the tub. "'Tis true, milord. I am responsible for Andrew's death."

CHAPTER EIGHTEEN

GEOFFREY STOOD, HIS frame looming in the doorway. Tall. Dark. Unyielding. Marsaili swallowed. Hard. A frisson of unease shivered down her spine.

"Get out of the bath. Now. We need to talk."

He disappeared into the bedroom and Marsaili climbed from the tub, wrapping her hair in a length of linen as she quickly dried off. She glanced about, finding a wrap hanging on a hook by the door. She slipped her arms into the voluminous sleeves and draped the soft, heavy fabric about her, belting it securely at her waist. Beatrice bounded to her feet as though she anticipated something exciting.

Marsaili shook her head at the dog. "This isnae going to be fun, wee dog. Ye may wish to stay in here."

Beatrice ignored the warning and pranced happily beside Marsaili as she entered the bedroom.

Lord de Wylde sat in one of the cushioned chairs

next to the hearth. His gaze bore into hers. Stern. Determined. Inflexible.

"Are ye judge *and* executioner?" she asked. Her knees shook.

He motioned to the empty chair. "Sit. Please."

Marsaili made it to the chair without incident and seated herself gracefully, sweeping the luxurious wrap about her, conscious of the rasp of the fabric against her bare skin. She unbound her hair and let it drape over her shoulder, finger combing the long strands before the fire.

"Shall we start from the beginning?" Lord de Wylde asked, his tone smooth. Calm. Steel.

Marsaili raised a brow. "Ye want to know how I killed Andrew?"

Lines tightened across his brow, giving her the only indication he was disturbed by her words.

"Did you kill him? Marsaili, it would help if you told me the entire story."

She gave him an angry shrug. "Why? 'Tis apparent yer English king is on Edmund's side. Edmund wouldnae have come here without the writ you asked for." Belligerence kept her tears at bay, for she knew Lord de Wylde had no choice but to hand her over to

Edmund. His code would not allow him to defy his king, and the truth would only make him despise her.

"I have my reasons," he said. "—which I will share with you after I hear your side of the tale."

Marsaili studied him intently. His amber eyes were dark. Hard. Compelling.

She'd trusted him once. Dare she try again?

She had nothing left to lose.

Geoffrey begged her silently. *Give me one good reason—any reason at all to be your champion.*

"I will not turn you over to Edmund. No matter what you tell me, the Bishop alone has the right to decide your fate."

Her eyes glowed with sudden tears. "'Twas not intentional."

He leaned forward and clasped her hands in his. "Then tell me."

Beatrice whined and leapt into Marsaili's lap, sparking a small smile as Marsaili pulled from Geoffrey's grip and helped the dog cuddle in the folds of fabric. Geoffrey settled back in his chair, his muscles relaxing somewhat from their tension. She wasn't making this easy on him.

"Andrew and Edmund had entered an argument.

Edmund lost his sword and grabbed another from a display on the wall. Truly furious, Edmund plunged the sword into Andrew's side, though it appeared an accident. For days, Andrew languished, feverish, dying. I'm no healer, but I remained at his side, wiping his brow, spooning broth between his lips. After more than a sennight, he awoke."

Geoffrey frowned. "I thought he died."

Marsaili glanced down, fingers plucking at Beatrice's wiry fur. "He remained verra weak for many days. 'Twas difficult for him to draw a full breath. He seemed to fight through this, and began to take a bit of exercise, slow steps across the room. He couldnae manage the stairs—he collapsed the only time he attempted it. He took over my solar above stairs, and I moved my things to replace his on the ground floor. For a time, he remained about the same and dinnae worsen."

"Were the two of you in accord?" *Forgive me, Marsaili, but I have to ask.*

She sent him a hard look. "We lived our lives separate for the most part. After two years with no children, there was nothing to hold us together other than our vows." She shrugged. "We dinnae hate each other, though I can say I dinnae miss him much."

Her sharp tone tugged at his heart. She had been trapped between a loveless marriage and a man who coveted his brother's title. "What happened?"

"He and Edmund spent much time closeted together. I heard Edmund more than once demand Andrew turn the title over to him, citing poor health. Andrew wasnae of Edmund's warring temperament, but he was stubborn. There were great shouting matches in the solar, and I believe his arguments with Edmund exhausted him."

"That does not explain why you say you killed him."

"'Twas a few days after one such episode that Andrew called me to him. He said he'd kicked the metal brazier that heated the room and broke his toe. 'Twas a horrible color—black and red and green—and verra swollen. I had the healer attend him, but the toe became putrid and nothing helped."

Marsaili's skin blanched. "Angry streaks of red flamed upward, followed soon by the green and black of dying flesh. Andrew knew what was happening. He knew it would eventually consume him. He knew his death wouldnae be pleasant. The healer wanted to amputate his foot. He refused." She sent Geoffrey a pleading look.

"He begged me to kill him."

HE BEGGED ME.

Damn! Did it excuse her actions, or was she responsible for murder? Geoffrey mulled over her words, viewing them from every possible angle.

I wouldnae agree. I couldnae end his life, though he pleaded with me daily. The healer mixed a concoction for me to administer when he became hysterical, and it sent him into a deep sleep. Thank God, it gave him rest.

She alone had been responsible for Andrew's care. Edmund had shunned the sickroom, though the smell alone could have driven the most stalwart away. Andrew became demanding, panicky, prone to violent bursts of temper. Not the man remembered by most. The entire castle reeled from the lord's impending death and the heavy drinking binges Edmund indulged in, knowing the lordship would soon be his.

Sometimes I gave Andrew the potion three or four times a day. 'Twas no time at all before his waking moments were filled with bitterness. He called me a coward. Uncaring. Glad to see him suffer. 'Twas not true. I couldnae wish such a death on anyone.

Geoffrey recalled the endless days she'd chattered at his bedside, coaxing Beatrice to show him her new tricks, engaging Simon or Walter in witty debate. He'd never met a more caring person than Marsaili. She was compassionate. Concerned.

He became withdrawn. Irritable. Feverish. I fetched another potion, but when I returned, he was already in a deep sleep. I placed the mug on the table beside him.

I escaped the room. 'Twas heaven to breathe the fresh air on the battlements. I knew my clothing and hair stank from endless hours in the sickroom. I knew Andrew would wake soon and become frantic if I wasnae there. But I stayed away until dark.

When I returned to Andrew's room, he was dead.

"What does yer Church say about assisting a suicide?" she asked.

Lord de Wylde remained silent for a few moments. "You did not kill Andrew." His words flat. Final.

Marsaili's throat was raw with unshed tears, swollen with the remembered horror of what she'd done.

"Edmund entered the room a moment later. My hand was on the mug. It took him less than a second to inform me he'd heard Andrew ask me for a potion to hasten his death. He accused me of poisoning Andrew."

She lifted her shoulders in a weary shrug. "Mayhap I did. I prayed every day for his end to come. I'd considered the potion the healer mixed. Wondered what would happen if he drank too much."

"Just because Edmund said you poisoned Andrew does not mean you did. And his word alone will not convict you."

Marsaili sent him a withering look. "Not in a court, but who's to say I would be tried by the king's man?"

"Edmund had no right to deny you justice!" Geoffrey rumbled, his face red.

"He thought so!" Marsaili flung back. "Andrew died four months ago. I spent almost two months in his stinking dungeon, begging for food. Light. Someone to talk to."

Geoffrey leaned forward and caught her upper arms in his hands and dragged her into his lap, perched across his good leg. She fought him, then sagged into his embrace, crying bitterly. Beatrice leapt to the floor, attaining the bed in one effortless bound. Geoffrey smoothed a hand over Marsaili's hair, repeating the motion until she was fairly drugged with the gentle caress.

"There was an investigation," she hiccupped. "Andrew's death was ruled a suicide. I know 'twas an accident. If I hadnae left the mug where he could reach it . . . ."

"He wasn't in his right mind, Marsaili. He was dying and afraid. I've seen battle-hardened men quail at the thought of amputation. Neither he nor you are to blame."

Marsaili sighed. "It doesnae matter. Edmund has sworn a warrant for me. He is prepared to hang me if I dinnae capitulate and marry him."

"How do you know this?"

She lifted her face. "Edmund visited me in the dungeon on three separate occasions. He told me Andrew had been buried at night, face down, a stake driven through his heart to anchor his spirit to this world. He said if I did not agree to marry him, he would have me convicted as a co-conspirator with Andrew. For my crime against God and the Church, I would receive the same treatment."

Geoffrey placed gentle fingers under her chin, his thumb caressing her cheek. "You are safe here. Never doubt that. He cannot harm you and I will not turn you over to him."

"You kept me here until he could come for me," she accused, though the words had lost much of their validity.

"Nay. I did not think he would actually go this far. And even if he did, he could not accuse the wife of a baron."

"What do you mean?" Marsaili's head began to spin as exhaustion dulled her mind.

"I mean, sweet Marsaili, when you ran from Edmund two days ago, I was only moments away from asking you to marry me."

CHAPTER NINETEEN

MARSAILI STARED AT him. "Ye'd ask me to marry ye?"

Geoffrey shook his head and eased her to her feet. "No."

"Not now?" she sneered, shame recoiling into anger.

Geoffrey rose, standing a bare hand's breadth from her, making her crane her neck to see his face. "'Tis not that easy, now."

"Ye will offer me sanctuary, but not yer name," she mocked. "The Saint has his code to live by. He always does the right thing." Her voice rose, scathing. "It would not be proper to sully his name with a woman who—"

With a muted roar, Geoffrey gripped her upper arms and jerked her against his body. His mouth slanted across hers, stilling her bitterness, commanding her to silence. Listen. Feel.

Sparks burst through her at his touch, igniting a desire that reverberated through her veins. Rising on her toes, she arched against him, pressing her body to his, demanding he feed the hunger he ignited.

She cupped his face in her hands. He shoved his hands inside her wrap, loosening it. The velvet rasped her sensitive skin, and she shrugged it off her shoulders. Geoffrey snatched the belt free and the fabric sagged to the floor, disregarded. His hands prowled her skin, sparking streaks of passion low in her belly. He circled his thumbs on her nipples, his touch tightening them beyond enduring. Marsaili mewled, sliding one knee along his hip as she pressed closer.

He gathered her against him, his breath harsh in her ears. His hands splayed across her back, his motions slow, gentling. Marsaili shattered as he pulled away.

"Then let me go home," she whispered, knowing she could not stay and deny the attraction between them. And she would not stay and be his mistress.

To her surprise, he grinned at her.

"'Tis not easy, because I would not know if you married me because you love me or because you merely wished to escape the hangman's noose."

Marsaili gasped. "'Tis no way to jest!"

"Look at it from my standpoint, milady. I could marry you—but at what concession from you? I do not wish to ponder your motives." He brushed lightly at the bulge in the front of his breeches, and Marsaili quirked an eyebrow, impressed. He gave her a searing look and a quick kiss, then grabbed his cane.

She fisted her hands on her bare hips, eyes narrowed in suspicion. "Where are ye going?"

"To talk to Edmund."

GEOFFREY WAS ABLE to pull himself away from Marsaili only with steely determination he hadn't experienced in many months. Though Marsaili hadn't exactly argued with him about becoming his wife, she had taken his hesitation poorly and there was only one thing he could do about it. Dispense with Edmund's obsession once and for all. He could then return and put the question of marriage to her in no uncertain terms. Perhaps taking up where they left off . . . .

He nodded to the pair of guards in the hall outside Marsaili's door and continued to the stair, maintaining a steady, careful tread on the worn stone. Simon appeared at the foot of the stairs, his face first register-ing surprise, then unease.

"How fares Milady?" he asked.

"She is in a bit of a tear," Geoffrey admitted.

Simon fell into slow step with him. Geoffrey passed the head of the stairs and continued to his rooms. Bracing his cane against the chair, he dragged his chain mail from its stand. Simon assisted solemnly, though Geoffrey could tell he barely contained his questions. At last Geoffrey relented.

"She alone nursed her late husband who suffered from a gangrenous toe. He begged her to help him die on more than one occasion." Geoffrey shrugged the surcoat into a better fit across his shoulders and reached for his gauntlets.

"She left the healer's potion within reach and 'tis her reasoning he drank it too soon, not knowing its effects. Whether he drank it on accident or not, Edmund accused her of assisting his brother to his death."

Geoffrey disbanded the splint on his leg and cast it aside. "He locked her in a cell for nearly two months whilst he mocked her with tales of Andrew's burial as a suicide. When she did not succumb to his offer to take her as his wife, he threatened to hand her over to the Church as a criminal."

"My God!" Simon exclaimed, his face infused with color. "I will settle him!"

Geoffrey buckled his sword across his hip. "No. I will."

><<

MARSAILI GLARED AT the closed door. "Ye amadan! Ye cannae fight Edmund! He doesnae fight fair!"

She snatched the wrap from its pile on the floor and flung it about her shoulders. After a moment's hesitation, she threw it across the bed and knelt before one of the clothing chests, rummaging through the contents.

"Ha!" Grabbing a dark blue bliaud edged in gold braid, she hurriedly dressed, pulling a matching surcoat over the top. She shoved her feet into a pair of slippers, sparing her ruined boots a rueful glance. Beatrice bounced from one side of the bed to the other as Marsaili rushed about.

Marsaili shoved her hair from her face, strands falling down her back in half-dry curls. Bending across the covers to ruffle Beatrice's furry head, she whispered, "Wish me luck!"

The little terrier barked her encouragement as Marsaili dashed from the room, startling the two guards who had clearly expected her to remain within. She disregarded their shouts, nimbly avoiding them as they thundered after her.

Sliding once in the soft slippers, Marsaili regained her footing and flew down the stairs, one hand trailing along the curved stone wall for balance. She burst into the great hall, scarcely able to stifle a shriek as Walter reached from the shadows and caught her wrist.

"Easy, Milady. The Saint asked me to watch for you. 'Tis best you are not a part of this."

Marsaili paused to catch her breath. "Part of what? And why do ye not help him?"

"He knew you would not listen to the other knights should they attempt to detain you."

She arched a brow at him in astonishment, aware of the huffs of the guards behind her. "But I will listen to ye?"

Walter gave his slow grin. "Aye, Milady. You will."

Though she knew Walter would not lay a hand on her, she balked at outright defiance of the man who had done nothing but help her since they'd met.

"Mayhap we could find a spot where we could watch?" she suggested.

"The battlements are chilly this eve, but you would be out of sight. 'Twould be best you not distract Lord de Ville."

Swallowing hard against sudden fear, Marsaili allowed Walter to usher her through the narrow hallways to the battement overlooking the gate. Below, the barbican shielded a number of soldiers as they marched in one side and out the other. Just beyond the gate, on the far side of the moat, an impressive array of armed men flanked two knights in chain mail which glowed in the fading light.

Simon and Geoffrey.

A burly man, made stouter by the swirling movements of his cape about his generous body, faced them, his own personal guard at his shoulder.

Edmund.

Behind him stood the men beneath Bellevue's banner, though there was not a face she could recognize from this distance.

"Will they fight, Sir Walter?" she asked, apprehension lacing her voice.

"I do not believe so," he replied casually. "'Tis not

Milord's intent."

"What is his intent?"

"Why, to see your name cleared, Milady."

"He is dressed to fight," she worried aloud.

"Aye. The Saint is always prepared."

Marsaili leaned her hands against the cold stone wall. Her surcoat flapped about her in the evening breeze. In the distance, the hills no longer carried the dull hues of winter, but boasted the palest greens and pink, darkened by the setting sun. In a matter of days, the lambs would begin their noisy entries into the world, heralding new life.

But tonight, in the shadows of the castle walls lurked the promise of death.

TORCHLIGHT ON THE ramparts brightened about her as darkness fell, but cast little light below. In growing frustration, Marsaili peered into the gathering gloom until she could no longer distinguish the men on the field. Her ears caught the groan of the portcullis chain and the creak of leather. Muted shouts rang out and Marsaili gripped Walter's arm.

He smiled. "They are within, milady. We may go

down, now."

With a low shriek of pent-up anxiety, Marsaili snatched up her skirts and fled down the narrow passageways to the great hall below.

Men filed into the room, chatting easily among themselves. Their swagger bespoke a conflict easily won. Marsaili scanned the area, her gaze lighting on Lord de Wylde as he and Simon approached the dais. As though he felt her presence, Geoffrey glanced up, meeting her look with a grin and a faint nod.

Ignoring the others in the room, she wove through their midst, her focus solely on Geoffrey. His smile widened and she flung herself into his arms, her hands capturing his cheeks to bring his lips down to hers.

A cheer went up and she ended the kiss, one hand against his neck as she touched her forehead to his.

"All is well, Marsaili," he murmured. "Now I believe we have business to discuss. In private, if you please."

Aware of the interest from the soldiers and servants alike, Marsaili nodded, but her body trembled and she could scarce let go of him. He clasped her hands gently and brought them to his lips, giving them each a gentle kiss. The roar of approval was unmistakable and

Marsaili's skin heated. With a steadying breath, she cocked her head at Lord de Wylde.

"Let us be about it, then," she said. Head tilted, a faint smile on her lips as she anticipated their private discussion, she moved through the crowd and up the stairs.

CHAPTER TWENTY

G EOFFREY ENDURED THE good-natured clouts to his shoulders and back as he attempted to follow Marsaili. Frustration with his shortened gate evaporated as his gaze riveted on her trim back, red hair tumbling to her waist, a slight swing to her hips. He grinned. He may have been several feet behind her, but the view was worth the delay.

The door to Geoffrey's bedroom snicked closed, sending Marsaili's heart rate into double time. Geoffrey divested himself of his gauntlets in a maddeningly casual fashion.

"Tell me what happened," she demanded.

He motioned to his surcoat. "Help me with this, please. I cannot remove it by myself."

She helped him undress, impatience warring with the sudden need to touch him as he replaced his mail with a soft linen tunic. Her fingers glided over his skin, smooth and warm. His gaze caught hers and she heated at his perusal.

"Do you wish to hear what was said, or shall we discuss other things?"

She whirled away and perched on the edge of the chair, out of reach. "Tell me what happened."

"I gave Edmund his horse back, though he bemoaned its abbreviated mane and tail," Geoffrey teased with a grin. Marsaili rolled her eyes and drew a deep breath of frustration.

"And he gave up his complaint against you."

She stared at him. "As simple as that?"

Geoffrey tilted his head side-to-side, a twinkle in his eyes. "Almost."

Marsaili leveled her gaze at him and tucked her hands beneath the edges of her surcoat where they would be less tempted to betray her need to touch him.

He sat on the edge of the hearth, right leg next to the banked embers, one hand dangling casually over his bent knee. "I was skeptical of Edmund's ability to obtain a writ from King Henry. Henry has his faults, among them the dislike to be embroiled in what he deems petty problems among his barons. Unless Edmund was a court favorite of Henry's, it seemed unlikely he could have gotten his attention long enough to request a writ for your capture."

"You knew this?"

Geoffrey shrugged. "I suspected. I was a knight at court for many months whilst training under my uncle who was the king's champion. I did not remember Edmund—or a Lord de Ville."

The corners of Marsaili's lips tilted upward. "I dinnae suppose Edmund knew this."

"He was a bit discouraged to discover Lord de Wolfe is my uncle and that I have attended the king. He was even more distressed to know I have seen the king's signature. And it does not match the scrawl on the writ."

Marsaili's eyes widened. "But, that's . . . ."

"Treason." Geoffrey supplied the word. "To Edmund's complete dismay, he cannot prove you poisoned Andrew. He also cannot prove Andrew took the concoction intentionally, though that will do Andrew little good." He held up his hand, two fingers bent. "He cannot pursue this matter with any hope I'd overlook his treasonous action." He lowered another finger. "And now, Milady, comes the last question. Would he dare charge the fair wife of Lord de Wylde?"

"He wouldnae," she whispered, staring at the finger

he leveled at her.

"Then, Lady Marsaili, do you consent to be my wife, without coercion or thoughts of gratitude for my actions on your behalf?"

Marsaili held back the rush of happiness. "Would ye often go to battle? I dinnae like war."

"I cannot promise you there will not be war. I will not stand idly by and give others freedom to harm my people. But I have no need to create war. 'Twas not that long ago that I determined to live a life of a monk, in peace, setting aside strife." He sighed. "'Twas admittedly before I met you."

Marsaili laughed in protest. "Milord, I am a peaceable woman!"

He rose and pulled her from her chair. "I am fascinated by you, Marsaili. I want to be amused by you, excited, astounded and loved by you for the rest of my life."

"We've spent the past weeks together, yet I scarcely know ye," she sighed. "I wish—"

Geoffrey pressed a fingertip to her lips. "I am grateful for those weeks. We already know what happens when we are left unchaperoned. I learned much about you in our time together—listening to you, watching you. I am encouraged to know that I will not wake one day after a night of intense passion and find I have no idea who I married."

Marsaili leaned against him. "Intense passion?" she queried, suddenly breathless.

"Shall I show you?" he murmured against her ear. His words tumbled through her in a sensuous slide, weakening her knees, sending pinpricks of heat along her skin. He tilted her head to receive his kiss, slanting his mouth across hers as he took possession of her soul. With a sweep of his hands, he divested her of her surcoat. His nimble fingers loosened the laces to her gown, tugged it off her shoulders.

With a wiggle, Marsaili freed the gown past her breasts and Geoffrey slid his palms down her sides, sending the bliaud over her hips and to the floor. She relished the feel of his hard frame as he hauled her against him. Her fingers widened the opening at the neck of his tunic and she slid her hands beneath the fabric, baring his shoulders to her caress.

She gave his skin her attention, nipping the line of his neck, the tip of her tongue gliding over the corded smoothness. Her palms slipped over his frame, relishing the rigid planes of his muscles. Sleek.

Powerful. Hers.

His hands lit fires within her, spurring her on. Encouraging. Tantalizing. She slid her fingertips beneath the waistline of his breeches, instantly encountering the tip of his erection. The heel of her hand slipped down its length and back up as a groan rumbled through his chest.

Moving his breeches quickly over the head of his cock, she pulled them down his long, muscular legs. Sinking before him, she unlaced his boots and he stepped out of them, then finished her task of removing his breeches. With a sinuous weave of her body, she gave languid attention to his cock as she slowly rose.

Geoffrey's hands clenched on her shoulders as he dragged her to her feet.

"You did not answer my question," he growled, nipping at the curve of her jaw.

"Which one?" she breathed.

"Will you marry me?"

She nodded. "Without coercion." She ran her tongue along the curve of his ear. "Without thought of what ye did for me today." She cupped the base of his cock in her hand, rubbing her thumb across the taut skin. "Only this."

Geoffrey backed her toward the bed, her knees crumpling as she sank onto the mattress. He eased down beside her, cursing the pain in his leg as he rolled onto his side. He fell to his back with a wry grin. "I don't believe my *cirurgian* would approve the normal position."

Marsaili tilted her head, interest on her face. "What do ye suggest?"

"Have you ever set the pace, milady?"

"In truth, I have received more pleasure at yer hands than ever from Andrew and his cock. I am eager to learn, milord."

Geoffrey's cock swelled tighter at her words. At his bidding, Marsaili sank over him, clutching his shoulders as if she were astride an untried horse for the first time. Geoffrey grinned. Then he groaned.

She hovered over him, setting her willing lips to his, and he tangled his hands in her hair, aflame with desire that demanded quenching. He settled one palm on her buttock, urging her on, and she arched her back, inviting his caress. Her movements quickened, her lips parted. Geoffrey fought for control as he teetered on the edge of release. He flattened his palms on the bed linens, certain he would lose his mind.

"Geoffrey!"

Her breathless cry pierced the fog in his head and he shouted at the intensity of his release, joining her as she gasped and shuddered.

She drooped to his chest and he stroked her back in aimless patterns. His breathing eased and his heartbeat slowed to a more normal pace. Tiny jolts of pleasure shot through his cock each time she clenched around him. Finally her spasms ceased.

With a sigh, she slipped to his side and nestled her head on his shoulder. She splayed her palm across his chest, fingers tangling in the mat of hair. "I am glad I took shelter in the auld barn that night," she murmured.

"Even though I changed your plans?"

"Even though ye caused me great delay, thinking ye are always right. Waylaying me on my journey to Scotland."

Geoffrey grinned and kissed the top of her head. "Shall we let the priest settle things?"

Marsaili ran the tip of a finger down the center of his chest. "What would ye have done had I truly been responsible for Andrew's death?"

Geoffrey cupped her cheek with his palm. "A true murderess—one who has no regrets for her actions, and no respect for life—must be dealt with. But, my love, in these past weeks I have seen in you only compassion and an esteem for others. Your past is not of your making, and we will create a future full of love and trust."

"Ye trust me? Even knowing my error caused a man's death?"

"We will take it as a solemn warning to not leave such potions within reach of an invalid." He settled onto his back. "Do you trust me?"

She sighed. "Though yesterday I believed ye had betrayed me, I see I was wrong. Ye could never do such a thing."

"I regret it took a dunk in a bog to bring you back to me."

"Aye. I regret the dunking as well."

Geoffrey laughed aloud. "I believe we will get along well together, Marsaili."

Her body grew lax in his arms. "Aye. We will." She yawned. "Send for yer priest. I have discovered something to keep me in England."

"What is that, my love?"

A languid smile tugged at the corners of her lips as she nestled closer.

"This."

EPILOGUE

Lockardebi, Scotland, just over the border
One week later

HEW'S LEGS TREMBLED as he slid from the back of the cart. The driver gave a grunt and a nod at the elder's mumbled thanks before clucking to his team and driving away. The gate to the keep was shut tight, the tower house beyond rising from the silent yard.

What in God's name has happened? Blearily, Hew eyed the unwelcoming sight. What had happened to the de Carlyles? Where was Marsaili and her family?

Dread settled in Hew's empty stomach, twisting painfully. Surely Edmund hadn't followed her all the way across the border. But why would the tower house seem abandoned?

He whirled, seeking the man who had dropped him at the gate, suddenly uncertain he wished to be here after all. But the cart dropped out of sight over a ridge, and Hew's old legs had no hope of catching up with the conveyance.

With trepidation, he trudged along the far side of the wall until he reached a small wooden gate set at an unobtrusive angle in the stone. He picked up a nearby stick and rapped on the square postern gate. With a squeak of rusty hinges, the narrow door swung open.

Hew shivered, both from the cold and from anxious expectation. What lay beyond the gate? Friend or foe? Mayhap a ghost?

Watery sunlight fell across Hew's shoulders and landed a few inches inside the partially open door. Beyond was dark as the maw of hell. Hew swallowed nervously.

"Hullo?" His voice squeaked upward, changing the challenge to a question. Silence answered. Hew took a hesitant step backward, gathering himself to flee.

"Dinnae trip over yer feet." A feminine voice drifted through the opening.

Hew froze.

"Iseabal?" He strained to hear a response, half afraid of what he'd find if he opened the door farther.

A face appeared out of the gloom and Hew staggered back. The lass sighed. "Come in, and dinnae act as if ye've seen a ghost. The only one here is tucked away in his shroud and not likely to harm anyone ever again."

Iseabal's eyes teared up at the sight of her sister's man-servant. The strain of the past weeks had taken its toll, and she felt as if one kind word, even a kind look or a compassionate tilt of the head, would shatter her carefully constructed wall of indifference.

No one had dared answer the summons at the gate, but she'd heard the knock as she crossed the empty bailey on her return from the chapel set against the wall surrounding the tower house.

Had Marsaili answered her missive? Though she'd begged her sister to travel with all haste, even with the hounds of hell behind her, she could not have arrived this quickly. And, truth be told, Iseabal hadn't been certain her sister would read her letter, much less ride here and provide aid.

She peered past auld Hew but saw naught but a blanket of fresh fallen snow arranged like fluffy sheep atop rocks and boulders and across low-hanging branches.

Her breath hitched. "Are ye alone? Is Marsaili not

with ye? Or Flore?" Surely Hew's sweet wife, who'd been the girls' nurse almost since their birth twenty-three years ago, would have come to help. But Iseabal had heard from neither Hew nor Flore, or Marsaili for that matter, in the years since her sister's marriage to the English baron.

"Aye," Hew said. His eyes cut away, as if reluctant to fully answer her question.

"Did ye get my letter?" she asked.

"Nae." He shook his head. "We've nae heard from ye these past years."

His hands gripped his elbows, hugging them to his skinny frame, reminding Iseabal of the cold.

"Come inside," she bade, motioning him through the gate. She closed and locked the door, pocketing the heavy metal key. Closing a hand over Hew's forearm, she halted his steps.

"I must warn ye," she said, capturing his attention. "Ye have noted the lack of soldiers on the wall." She waited for Hew's nod.

"I thought the keep was deserted," he admitted.

Weariness drew Iseabal's shoulders down as she remembered those who had escaped the keep no more than three days prior.

"It nearly is," she confessed. "Da went out reiving a month back and returned with the hounds of de Wolfe on his heels."

Hew's aged, parchment skin blanched.

"The keep held for a sennight or so, but the English tunneled beneath the wall to the north." She glanced over her shoulder as if she could see the damage from the postern gate. Thankfully she couldn't, but the thundering crash of the huge stones and the screams of women and dying men still rang in her ears.

"Da was struck by a portion of the wall, and, when he regained consciousness a few hours later, the English had already burned us out."

Iseabal wrung her hands. "There are only a few of us left. The men were either killed or taken away. They wanted to hang Da, but I begged them not to. Seeing him so close to death, their leader agreed." Tears stung the backs of her eyes, startling her when she thought she'd shoved her emotions deep inside.

"After stripping us of food and water and anything else they could manage, they left."

"Left ye alone?" Hew asked, indignant lines drawing his body up sharply. "With yer da dying? How many are left?"

"Six, counting me," Iseabal replied. "Though the others are likely to bolt as soon as Da draws his last breath. I sent Marsaili a letter as soon as I could, hoping she would make the journey and find peace before Da passes." She peered past the auld man. "Why is she not with ye?"

Hew shook his head. "I lost her," he mourned.

Iseabal flinched. "Lost her?" she countered.

"Her husband died a little more than a month past. Her brother by marriage, a brute of a man who doesnae deserve to draw breath, kept her locked away, threatening to accuse her of Lord Andrew's death and petition the king for her arrest if she dinnae marry him."

"That's against the law!" Iseabal exclaimed.

Hew shrugged. "I dinnae ken the way of the English nobles, but if she'd agreed, attention wouldnae have been drawn to the marriage, legal or no'."

Iseabal gripped Hew's sleeve. "Where is she?"

"She escaped a sennight ago—me with her. Her horse went lame outside of a wee village called Appleton. She agreed we should wait out the storm at the inn, but when I went back outside after securing rooms, she was gone."

Iseabal's hand flew to her throat. "She went on alone? Or do ye suspect foul play?"

"I dinnae ken," Hew mourned. "'Twas another conveyance in the yard when she left. I pray she dinnae fall afoul of those men."

"Who were they, Hew?" She tugged urgently on his arm. "Tell me!"

"The verra worst, milady," Hew said, his face twisted in fear and grief. "'Twas the rogue known as The Saint."

THE END

Acknowledgments

I would like to thank Kathryn le Veque for inviting me to be a part of this wonderful opportunity to write in her World of de Wolfe series. It was my first foray into England as a writer, and the process was immense fun! I am thrilled to be among such wonderful authors!

Thanks go to my fantastic critique group, Cate Parke, Dawn Marie Hamilton, and Derek Dodson, who helped keep me on the right path as Marsaili sassed her way through the English countryside and Lord de Wylde lost his distinctly stuffy attitude and became a man worth loving.

FROM THE AUTHOR

Thank you so much for your interest in The World of de Wolfe! I hope you are enjoying the series and that it will encourage you to read more books by the authors in this group. Please consider leaving a review for the books you enjoy. It helps more than you know!

I love hearing from readers! You can 'follow' me on Amazon, or Facebook, Instagram with #cathymacrae_ author, or Pinterest. Spend a bit of time wandering through my website. You can read about books, authors and the writing process on my Bits 'n Bobs blog, or find out a bit more about me, my dogs and gardening on my Wonderful Wednesday blog. Connect with me via my address cathymacrae@ cathymacraeauthor.com. And if you'd like to keep up via a newsletter and discover new books, promotions, and other fun, you can sign up on my website at www.cathymacraeauthor.com.

More Books by Cathy MacRae

The Highlander's Bride Series:

The Highlander's Accidental Bride (Book 1)

The Highlander's Reluctant Bride (Book 2)

The Highlander's Tempestuous Bride (Book 3)

The Highlander's Outlaw Bride (Book 4)

The Highlander's French Bride (Book 5)

With DD MacRae

The Hardy Heroines series

Highland Escape (book 1)

The Highlander's Viking Bride (book 2)

The Highlander's Crusader Bride (book 3)

The Highlander's Norse Bride, a Novella (book 4)

The Ghosts of Culloden Moor series

with other authors

Adam (book 11)

Malcolm (book 16)

MacLeod (book 21)

Patrick (book 26)

Made in the USA
Monee, IL
12 August 2024

63693634R00134